Caffeine Nights Publishing

Lincolnshire
COUNTY COUNCIL

discover libraries

This book should be returned on or before the due date.

NAM 2/18

14/11/2019

Published by Caffeine Nights Publishing 2016

Published in Great Britain by
Caffeine Nights Publishing
4 Eton Close
Walderslade
Chatham
Kent
ME5 9AT

www.caffeinenights.com

British Library Cataloguing in Publication Data.
A CIP catalogue record for this book is available from the British Library

ISBN: 978-1-910720-49-3

Also available as an eBook

Cover design by
Mark (Wills) Williams

Everything else by
Default, Luck and Accident

CHASING GHOSTS
'If you are not looking for something you don't see it.'

MICHAEL FOWLER

Michael Fowler was born and brought up in the Dearne Valley area of Yorkshire where he still lives with his wife.

At the age of 16 he left school with the ambition of going to art college but his parents' financial circumstances meant he had to find work and so he joined the police.

He has never regretted that decision, serving as a police officer for thirty-two years, both in uniform and in plain clothes, working in CID, and undercover in Vice Squad and Drug Squad, retiring as an Inspector in charge of a busy CID in 2006.

Since leaving, Michael has embarked on two careers: he is an established author with two crime series to his name: DS Hunter Kerr and DS Scarlett Macey, he has also co-written a true crime story.

He is a member of the Crime Writers Association and International Thriller Writers.

Michael has also found considerable success as an artist, receiving numerous artistic accolades. Currently his work can be found in the galleries of Spencer Coleman Fine Arts at Lincoln and Stamford.

Find out more at www.mjfowler.co.uk
or follow him on Twitter @MichaelFowler1.
Also Like Michael on Facebook.

Also by Michael Fowler

DS Hunter Kerr series

Heart of the Demon
Cold Death
Secrets of the Dead
Coming, Ready or Not
Black & Blue (e-book novella)

Scarlett Macey series
Scream, You Die!

True crime
Safecracker

FOREWORD

I have always had a passion for writing and twenty-something years ago I begun venturing to writers' groups to develop my writing skills. Those sessions brought about many experiments, lots of first chapters, short stories and also story lines and plots. The idea for this crime suspense thriller started out during one of those sessions in 1992. It was typed on a word processor, ran to just over 100 pages and was my first completed crime story. Then, like now, it was a novella and although the locations have changed and some characters have been added since that early piece, fundamentally, this story is the same. I hope you enjoy.

Michael Fowler

This is dedicated to my good friend Terry Wigley. I miss our chats.

1

The throbbing in his head started the moment he broke from sleep. In some discomfort, Toby Alexander rolled over and slowly opened his eyes. Without warning a torrent of intense sunlight flooded his vision, adding to the pain. Letting out a moan he threw up a hand for protection and slammed shut his eyelids. In that instance it felt like a jackhammer had started work on the back of his retinas and it made him feel sick. Letting out another soft whine he lay like that for several seconds waiting for the flashing stars to subside, wishing away his hangover. Then he flicked open his eyes for a second time. Judging by the brightness pouring through the central gap in the curtains, and given that it was early spring, he guessed it was either very late morning, or early afternoon. He made an attempt at sitting up. Suddenly he felt the atmosphere within the bedroom closing in and the room began spinning. Snapping shut his eyes again he took a deep breath and told himself to get a grip. It took him the best part of half a minute to stop the nausea and pull himself together, and then gingerly re-opening his eyes he kick-started his thoughts into remembering last night's events, especially how he got here. How had he got home? Nothing was filtering through into his aching head. He rolled over to Carrie's side to see how she was – to see if she could remind him, but her side of the bed was empty and, judging by the undisturbed pillows, it looked as though she hadn't slept there. The thought of her jarred his conscience, igniting a vortex of blurred images inside his head. They were fleeting but they were enough to jog his memory that they had argued … again. He cursed. Why did he do this? Why couldn't he control his temper? He knew he would be facing the silent treatment once more from Carrie and would have some serious making up to do. *There had been too many times of late.* Taking another deep breath, he flung himself into action, swinging his legs out over the bed. Starting to rise, he had to catch himself as light-headed dizziness engulfed him and he could feel sweat forming on his brow. He clawed for air and held the breath. Within twenty seconds the moment had passed and, easing himself up, he soft-footed out of the bedroom and onto the landing. The guest bedroom door was ajar and he peeked around to see if Carrie was asleep there. The room was empty – the bed didn't look as if it had been disturbed either.

She must have slept on the sofa.

Returning to the bedroom he noticed for the first time the tangle of his clothes on the floor beneath the window. Clothes he'd worn last night. Thin strips of soft light from the bottom gap in the curtains played on them and he could see they looked to be in a state. He picked up his jeans as if handling contaminated waste and ran his eyes over them. They were caked in mud and damp. *What on earth' happened? Where's this from?* He took another disgusted look at them and dropped them back on the pile. At the bottom of his bed were his boxers. He saw that these were unsullied, he pulled them on and ambled his way into the bathroom. Running the tap in the sink he gazed into the mirror. His skin was waxy and sheathed in perspiration. He looked shit. He felt shit. Swilling his face in cold water, he towelled and made his way downstairs. The lounge door was open and, although the room was in semi darkness because the heavy drapes were closed, he could see that the sofa was empty. He stood for a second and listened. The house was quiet. Sighing, he made his way into the kitchen-cum-diner. As he entered, a cool breeze met him, making him shudder, and he realised where it was coming from when he spotted that the rear door to the garden was open.

She must be getting some fresh air.

As he stepped into the kitchen he stood on something sharp which made him yelp, snapping up his foot he saw blood beginning to dot the flagstone floor. At the same time, he spotted fragments of broken glass and one of the dining chairs on its side. Another overwhelming sense of wooziness began to envelope him and he grabbed at the work surface to steady himself. He could feel his body breaking into a clammy sweat and he drew in a lungful of air and held it. Within a couple of seconds, the faint feeling had receded, and, exhaling slowly he took couple of hops to the sink where he turned on the tap and threw more cold water onto his face. He took another deep breath, balanced himself, and pulled up his leg to grab his ankle. Blood was dripping from beneath his foot, steady droplets splashing the floor. He twisted round his foot to view the injury. There was a gash close to his big toe, a small piece of glass embedded in the wound. Groaning, he reached for the tea towel, and with thumb and forefinger carefully prised out the shard, quickly binding up his foot with the towel as a globule of blood appeared in the slit. Twisting the loose ends into a tourniquet, he stared back to where he had stepped on the broken glass. Near to the upturned chair he spotted two damaged stems and, widening his gaze, he saw that a large area of the floor was littered with shards. He instantly realised it was the remnants of a couple of wineglasses he had stepped on. But then, what especially caught his eye was the dark red crusted stain covering one of the large Cornish stone flags. The puddle of congealed blood snapped him out of his languor.

2

Just what on earth's gone on here? He wondered, dragging back his eyes and knotting the towel as best he could around his foot. He stared at the fragments of glass scattered across the floor and took in the dried puddle-stain of blood again and tried to focus on last night. More ghostly images drifted into his thoughts. Now he could recall, some of their argument had been staged in the kitchen... but he didn't remember this happening.

What with this and the condition of his clothes upstairs. *Christ! What the bloody hell's happened?*

He pushed himself away from the work top he had been using as support and hobbled to the back door to look for Carrie. On the threshold a gentle but cold wind brushed his face as he explored the garden and vegetable patch. She wasn't there, and his gaze took him to the uneven and broken boundary hedgerow into the rolling meadow where it sloped toward Merthen Point. It was a place she regularly took herself to think – especially after a quarrel.

In the distance he could hear the Atlantic Ocean pounding Coffin Rock.

She was nowhere to be seen.

Closing the back door, he checked the towel bandage was still tight and, avoiding the broken glass, half-hopped, half-hobbled to the front door. He saw the key was in the lock on this side and he turned the handle. It was unlocked. He flung it open. There was only his car on the drive – Carrie's had gone.

She had done this before – steamed off in a huff, but usually she let him know about it with a dramatic display of temper. Sneaking off like this wasn't her style at all. Then he thought about the congealed blood in the kitchen and wondered if she'd taken herself to the hospital. It had to be that, he told himself, but he wanted to be sure, so he hopped upstairs to the bedroom where he checked her wardrobe and then the chest of drawers. All her clothing was there. He heaved a sigh of relief and dropped down heavily onto the edge of the bed.

More of their squabble was coming back to him – some of the hurtful things he'd hurled at Carrie. He also remembered taking the couple of wraps of cocaine which he'd washed down with wine when he was already drunk. He wondered if that's why he was having difficulty chaining last night's events together.

He shook his head. He'd screwed up again. *I can be such a bastard sometimes.*

He needed to check she was okay, so, returning to his crumpled and muddy jeans he hoisted them up and rifled through the soggy pockets for his mobile phone. Finding it, he brought up Carrie's contact tab and hit the phone image. He listened to it dialling out, willing her to answer. It rang for ten seconds before switching to voicemail. For a split-second he thought about leaving her a message – but then dismissed it – he would rather apologise to her personally so he ended the call and hit redial. It rang out again but was unanswered. He could feel himself getting agitated. Irritated, he typed 'Where are you', and was just about to send the text when he had second thoughts and added 'I'm sorry' before mailing it. For five minutes he sat on the edge of the bed staring at his mobile, waiting for a response, but none came.

This is just typical of her. Making him suffer like this!

Slinging his phone onto the pillow he decided to go for a soak in the bath to calm down. His head was still pounding.

3

Removing the towel, Toby saw that the wound had already began to clot and, scrutinising it further, determined that it wasn't too deep – the glass had gone in at an angle and it only required a plaster. Following a warm bath, he sought out the bathroom first aid box, applied treatment and made his way downstairs where he spent the remainder of the morning tidying up the kitchen – binning the broken glass, scrubbing away the dried blood, and washing his soiled clothes. In between he drank coffee and water to re-hydrate himself; he rang Carrie's phone, but she still didn't pick up.

By mid-afternoon his hangover was waning and he made himself a cheese sandwich and ate it slowly while watching television, but he found himself unable to focus - more of last night's fight had come back to him while he had been cleaning up and he was feeling ashamed and guilty. By five o'clock his guilt had changed to concern and, thinking about the bloodstain he had scrubbed up and bleached that morning, he decided to ring the hospital.

Penzance was the nearest one. He dialled the hospital switchboard and asked to be put through to the Accident & Emergency department where he enquired after Carrie Jefferies. He was told no one had come in of that name and he asked the receptionist to double-check. The answer was the same.

At 7p.m. and with a sense of frustration, he telephoned his friends James and Tammy Callaghan – it was at their house that he and Carrie had spent the previous evening. James answered.

"James it's Toby."

'I wondered when you'd ring.'

Toby caught a harsh tone in his friend's voice. He took a deep breath and said, 'I think I need to apologise.'

There was a moment's silence on the other end then James responded, 'Not to me you don't but I hope you have to Carrie, and it would be fair to say Tammy's not too impressed with you either.'

'Was I that bad?'

'Don't you remember?'

'I can't remember much of it at all, just a few snippets.'

'I'm not surprised. You were off your face by the end of the evening. You're lucky Carrie drove you home. Tammy wouldn't have done if it had been me.' There was another pause and then James added, 'What on earth got into you? I've seen you get pissed Toby, and argumentative, but last night was the worst I've seen you. Why did you go off on one like you did?'

For a moment Toby thought about what James had said but his answer was too long, and in any case it wasn't justification for the previous evening's outburst, so he replied, 'I don't know James. A culmination of a lot of things I suppose, but it's no excuse and so I apologise again.' Pausing he furthered, 'I hope we're still okay – you and I?'

'You and I are okay. As I say, Tammy was really pissed off because it spoilt a good evening, but it's Carrie we were worried about. You said some pretty nasty things to her.'

Toby pursed his lips, 'I know. She didn't deserve it.'

On a low note James responded, 'No she didn't. She's the best thing that's happened to you. You're going to end up losing her if you continue like that.'

Suddenly feeling downcast Toby answered, 'I know. In fact, I think she may already have dumped me.'

'What do you mean?'

'I haven't seen her all day and she's not answering my calls or texts. She'd gone by the time I woke up this morning and I've been trying to get hold of her. You haven't seen her have you? She hasn't turned up there, or spoken with you has she?'

'No she hasn't I'm afraid Toby.'

Toby sensed honesty in his friend's voice. He said, 'What about Tammy? Has she been in touch with her?'

'I don't think so. Just a minute, she's in the other room I'll ask.'

Toby heard James shout his wife's name, then his voice became muffled and he guessed he was holding his hand over the receiver. He heard Tammy's voice in the distance but couldn't make out what she was saying. A couple of seconds later James was back on the line.

'Sorry mate. Carrie's not rung here.' There was another short pause and then James asked, 'Don't worry she'll be back. It's not as though she's anywhere to go. I mean she doesn't have any family here and didn't she say that all her friends live back home in Australia.'

Toby nodded to himself, 'That's right, except for me, and you two of course, we're the only people she really knows.'

'Well she's definitely not rung us.' There was another pause and then he said, 'What about her stuff has she taken that?'

'She's gone off in her car but she's not taken any of her clothes. They're all still here.'

'Well I wouldn't worry then mate. She's gone off in a hissy and needs some breathing space. If she's not taken any clothes that means she'll be back. And if I was you, when she does come back, I'd have the biggest bunch of flowers waiting for her.'

'Toby took in a sharp intake of breath. Then he said, 'I guess you're right. I'll do that.' Then before he hung up, 'James if she does contact you or Tammy, you will let me know won't you?'

'Sure mate no probs. Give me a ring when you sort everything out.'

James hung up.

4

Toby was woken by the sound of wind and rain lashing the window panes. He'd not closed the curtains when he'd finally gone to bed just after midnight and his first view of what morning held was a sky laden with angry dark storm clouds. For a moment he lay there listening to the weather, staring beyond the casement window and, without warning, the thought of Carrie jumped back inside his head. He had slept fitfully – tossing and turning most of the night, his mind attempting to jigsaw the events of what had happened the previous evening, first at James and Tammy's, and then back here, but he had struggled to put a full sequence of actions together. He could recall the early part of the evening. He and James had especially got on well, as usual chatting about art and their work, but then the atmosphere changed at the dinner table. Carrie had triggered the mood change – his mood change - with her comment of, 'Do we have to listen to art again? Can't we just talk about something else?' He'd instantly reacted by sniping back, 'Why is it far too intellectual for you?' bringing scorn from Tammy, causing her to sulk. That's when he had thought *bugger the pair of them* and stepped up his drinking. By the end of the meal he was rounding on them, most of his conversation being sarcastic retorts that had resulted in Carrie telling him he'd drunk too much and she thought it was time for home. And that's when he had gone into meltdown – banging the table repeatedly and demanding, 'Who the fuck do you think you are, trying to control my life?' He could recall his foul language becoming a tirade and James and Tammy had come to Carrie's defence, which had made him even more angry, but beyond that everything was a jumble.

Following yesterday's telephone chat with James, he could vaguely bring to mind getting in the car with Carrie driving, but he couldn't remember the journey home, and as for whatever happened in the kitchen, that was nothing but a blur of gyred images thrashing around inside his head. How his clothes had got into that state, how the two wineglasses had got broken and where the blood had come from remained a complete mystery?

He closed his eyes and slapped his hands against the side of his head shouting 'Fuck' to an empty room. His life was a bloody mess again and he knew it was down to him.

Taking longer than normal in the shower, letting the warm jet ease away the tension in his neck, he ran through a battle plan as to what he needed to do that day, then he got dressed and made his way downstairs. Although his stomach was churning with emptiness he felt sick and knew he couldn't face anything to eat so he made himself a mug of coffee. While he waited for it to cool he made his first phone call. Carrie's mobile. It didn't ring out. It went straight to voicemail. She'd either switched her phone off or the battery was dead. He ended the call, staring at his mobile and cursed. Last night he'd left three messages and she hadn't got back. She always got back – even when pissed with him. Sure, she would let him suffer a few hours but she'd get back. He decided to call James and Tammy's again. Tammy answered. Taking a deep breath, he asked, 'I'm just checking if Carrie's been in contact since yesterday?'

On a tetchy note she responded, 'I'll put you on to James.'

Toby heard the phone being put down followed by Tammy's barely audible call to James and then a couple of seconds later the phone was picked back up.

'Hi mate. How are things?' James sounded lively.

'I'm just ringing to see if Carrie's got in touch since yesterday?'

'Sorry mate she's not rung here. She's not been in touch then? Not come back?'

Toby was staring at the kitchen window his wraithlike reflection stared back. He watched himself shaking his head. 'Nope. Nothing from her. Still not answering my calls. I checked the hospital at Penzance just in case she'd been in an accident but she's not there. I don't know what to do?'

'Have you rung the police?'

Toby's face changed. He caught the shocked look in his reflection. After a short pause he said sharply, 'No I don't want to bother them.'

'Well that's something I'd think about, especially if you don't track her down by the end of the day. As you said, about the accident. I don't want to scare you, but she could have crashed her car and be trapped somewhere, or she might be unconscious in a hospital and no one knows who she is. If I was you I'd give them a call. Put your mind at ease at least.'

Toby thought about what James had said and replied, 'Yeah I'll see how things go and if I've not heard anything from her by the end of the day I'll think about it.'

'To be honest Toby, if it was me, I'd do it as soon as.'

'I'm just going to do another check with the hospital.'

'Yeah okay. Let me know how you go on mate.'

Before ending their conversation Toby said, 'Tammy sounded a bit frosty with me.'

'I'm afraid you're really in her bad books at the moment but she'll come round.' After a short pause he added, 'Anyway, can't stand chatting, I'm guessing you've got loads of ringing round to do. As I say, let me know how you go on.'

Before Toby had time to respond James hung up.

Trance-like, Toby stared at the phone listening to the long burr. He knew he should take James' advice – contact the police and report Carrie missing, but that was something he dare not do. Not with his past.

5

Detective Constable Jack Buchan was slouched over his desk, running his eyes over the summary page of the court remand file he had freshly printed off when he felt a gentle tap on his shoulder. He stabbed a finger over the sentence he had just read, held it there and looked up. Detective Inspector Dick Harrison was leaning over him.

'Morning Jack.'

'Morning Boss.'

'Up to much?'

'Just going through the paperwork for last night's robbery. CPS want it by lunchtime – they're going for a remand.'

'Oh, you picked that job up then?'

'Yeah, everybody else was tied up.'

'And you okay with that?'

'Yeah sure. No problem. To be honest it's a cut and dried job. Caught at the scene and a straight up cough.

'Oh okay. It's Ryan Mason that's trapped up isn't it?'

Jack nodded. 'It certainly is, bless his little cotton socks. He's not a happy bunny. And that's not surprising given what happened to him.' He had to hold back an urge to smile as he finished the sentence. Ryan Mason was one of their regulars. Jack had dealt with him many times over the years. 'To be honest, the custody officers told me before I went in to interview him that Monkey had suffered a bit of a hiding. And not from the officers who turned out to the call but from the victim! It's the easiest interview I've ever done with him. I didn't have one 'no comment' from him this morning. It's amazing what a good hiding can do to loosen someone's tongue. Maybe it's something we should go back to?'

'Now, now, Jack, let's not go there. None of your Life on Mars stuff here.'

Jack let out a chuckle.

'I thought I'd read on the tagged incident that the complainant is a pensioner?'

'He is, but he's built like a barn door apparently. He's a retired coalman. Spent forty-odd years humping hundredweight sacks of coal about. Still as strong as an ox. Monkey went there armed with a baseball bat, but the bloke smacked him in the face before he could even take a swing, then he took the bat off him and gave him a good hiding with it. When the officers got there, Monkey was screwed into a ball screaming, "get him off me."'

'Some summary justice then?'

'Just a bit. He's had it a long time coming. He'll probably think twice now before he does his next job. And you ought to see Monkey's face. He was ugly enough before, but now his looks have been enhanced by a pair of walled up eyes and a broken nose.'

'So why did he do go to his house then?'

'He heard in the pub that the guy had a safe at his house with a load of cash in it. Thought because of the guy's age he'd be a pushover. You know what he's like – dense as fog in a Sherlock Holmes film. He just steamed in there without doing his homework.'

'And is there a safe at the man's house?'

'There is, but he's doesn't keep much in it these days – mainly paperwork – deeds to his house, that kind of thing. The safe was from when he had his coal business, but he's been retired ten years now – sold up to a local builder's merchants.'

'And you say CPS have suggested remanding Ryan?'

'Yeah they've recommended a charge of robbery. He was already on bail for assault. He smacked the landlord of the King Arms for refusing to serve him a couple of weeks back. He's probably going to get a good few years inside this time.' Jack broke into a grin. 'All the misery he's heaped on folks in the past, it couldn't have happened to a better man.'

The DI met Jack's self-congratulatory smirk with one of his own. 'Good job Jack. Good to have you back in the fold.' Then his face set straight, 'You okay?'

Jack offered a brief nod, 'Yes it's good to be back. I never thought I'd miss this shit-hole of a job but I did.'

Dick Harrison let out a laugh, 'Good to see you haven't lost your sense of humour.' Then he stepped to one side, 'I want to introduce you to our newest recruit.'

Directly behind the Detective Inspector stood a slim, dark haired, twenty-something female. She was dressed in a midnight blue trouser suit and white cotton blouse.

'This is Fabi – Fabi Nosenzo. She's here on attachment. She's wants to be a detective and I want you to show her the ropes.'

Jack Buchan pushed himself up from his desk and offered his hand. 'Fabi – what a lovely name.'

'It's short for Fabiola. My parents are Italian.' She took a step forward and clasped Jack's large hand.

Her grip was strong and confident. Jack held on to it momentarily, studying her features. Her hair was scraped back exposing high cheekbones and sparkling almond shaped eyes and her olive complexion was flawless. There was a fresh natural beauty about her that he couldn't help but admire and, as he viewed her, the term classic beauty instantly came into his thoughts. As he let go of her hand she offered up a smile, but Jack felt that it seemed forced, almost nervous, and he attempted to set her at ease by returning an avuncular grin, before saying, 'Welcome to CID Fabi. And by the way, that comment I made about this being a shit-hole of a job, just ignore me. I'm a typical cynical old detective. What I really meant was that this is a wonderful job, with good pay and conditions, the hours are great, and everyone loves you and regularly tells you how well you're doing.'

She let out a snort of laughter.

The DI switched his gaze between the seasoned and fledgling detectives. 'See I told you what to expect.'

Jack turned to the DI, 'Should I be offended by that comment?'

'On the contrary Jack I told her I was putting her with my best detective.'

'Now who's bullshitting?'

Dick Harrison let out a laugh, 'No flies eh Jack?' Then on a serious note he said, 'You know the drill Jack. Fabi's with us for six months at least. I want you to look after her and show her how the job should be done.'

Jack nodded, 'Sure boss.'

'And your first job together is waiting for you downstairs in the foyer. I've just been told a lady wants to report a friend missing and that she's concerned for her welfare. Uniform were going to deal with it but the lady insists on speaking to a detective. She thinks her friend may have come to some harm. Are you okay with that?'

'Yeah the Mason file is done. I'll e-mail it across to CPS and then we'll nip down and speak to her.'

6

The slip of paper in Jack Buchan's hand told him that Tammy Callaghan was 33 years old and that she lived in The Old Fisherman's cottage at Penberth Cove. The woman he was trading eye contact with in reception was petite with a bob of light brown hair framing a fresh looking face that bore only a hint of makeup.

She displayed an anxious look.

'Ms Callaghan, Tammy Callaghan,' he said stepping forward. He shook her hand, his hand almost swallowing her dainty one. Her shake was limp.

He told her his name and introduced Fabi. Then he said, 'We've been told you're concerned about a friend?'

She shied away her sparkling grey eyes. 'Yes I am. Carrie. She's gone missing and no one's heard a thing from her.'

'Carrie you say. What's her full name?

'Carrie Jefferies.'

'And how old is Carrie?'

Tammy canted her head and took on a thoughtful look. 'I think she's early thirties. I believe she's slightly younger than me.' She paused and glanced up. A couple of seconds later she returned her gaze. 'To be honest I'm not quite sure.'

'But you'd say roughly around the thirty mark?'

Tammy nodded.

'And when exactly did she go missing?' Jack asked.

'Sunday. Early hours Sunday morning was the last time I saw her. Five days ago now. She had a row with her boyfriend and since then we've not heard from her.'

'And you think she may have come to some harm?'

She returned her gaze. 'Well I'm not too sure. I don't want to get anyone into trouble. But, well, it just doesn't feel right. I mean it was an almighty row they had and now she's just disappeared. He says she's gone off on her own accord, but I'm not so sure. He had a lot to drink that night and he can be quite nasty when he's had a few.'

Jack touched her shoulder and pointed out one of the interview rooms in reception, 'I think we need to have a chat,' he said and guided her across the floor.

The small soundproof room they entered was only big enough for a table and four chairs. Tammy Callaghan took the chair offered her at the back of the narrow room and Jack and Fabi took up their places across the table.

Jack watched her pick her fingers for a few seconds then said, 'I can see you're nervous Tammy. May I call you Tammy?'

She stopped picking the skin around her cuticles, looked up and gave a quick nod.

'As I said, I can see you're nervous, but you've no need to be Tammy. You're here because you're concerned about a friend and you've every right to talk to the police. I'm sure if the roles were reversed your friend would be sat here doing exactly the same thing.'

'She's not really my friend.' She squeezed her eyes and a frown appeared, 'What I mean is she's a friend of sorts but not a good friend.' She paused, 'Am I making sense?'

Jack nodded, 'I understand. Now you said Carrie went missing five days ago?'

Tammy laid her delicate palms flat on the table. 'Yes, she and Toby…'

'Toby?' Jack interjected.

'Toby Alexander. That's who Carrie lives with. They came to our house for a meal and they ended up having this almighty row.' She straightened herself and switched her gaze between Jack and Fabi. 'Look, it's like I say I don't want to get anyone into trouble, but it's the circumstances in which she's gone that I'm not happy with.'

'I can see you're troubled Tammy. In your own words just take us through things and then we'll see if there's anything we need to worry about.'

Tammy took a deep breath 'Last Saturday evening Toby and Carrie came to our house for a meal. Toby is my husband's friend – he invited them. I know Carrie, not really that well, but she's a lovely person and easy to get on with. Well, we had a couple of drinks and had our meal and then just started chatting. It was all very friendly at first. We've had a couple of meals together before.

My husband and Toby got to chatting about art – like they usually do – they're both professional artists – and Carrie just made a comment about them "always talking about art. Can we talk about something else?" It was just a comment, but Toby took it really personal and started having a go at Carrie – calling her stupid and started picking on her. I tried to calm him down but he'd had quite a bit to drink and there was no calming him. He just got worse as the evening wore on and we ended up calling it a day just after midnight. Toby was quite smashed. In fact, he was having trouble standing and my husband had to help him into the car. Carrie was driving. I did ask her if she was going to be all right because he was still picking on her and she said that she was "used to him being like this" and then drove off. The next day Toby rang my husband and asked if we'd seen or heard from Carrie because she wasn't at home. To be honest, it didn't surprise me given the state he was in. I just thought good for her. But then he rang us on the Monday and told us he'd still not heard from her. My husband told him to report her missing to you but I don't know if he's done that. I've just come to see if you know about it and see if she's turned up or not. It's been five days now and she's not answering her mobile. I've left her a couple of messages on her voicemail and she's not come back to me. I'm really worried about her.'

'I'm not aware that she's been reported missing Mrs Callaghan. Her name doesn't ring any bells. Do you think she might have come to some harm then?' enquired Jack.

She nodded and then shrugged her shoulders. 'I know we're not the closest of friends but I just think she'd at least let me know she was all right.'

'And do you think her boyfriend Toby may have harmed her.'

She pursed her lips, 'He was in a bit of a state.'

Jack started to push himself up locking onto Tammy Callaghan's probing eyes. 'Tammy I want us to go to another room, there's a number of questions I want to ask you and I want to record it. Is that okay?'

7

As best he could, given that the chairs were hard plastic, Jack tried to make himself comfortable in the video interview room.

Fabi had got them all a hot drink from the machine along the corridor and passed three compressed paper cups filled with unappetizing looking coffee around the desk.

Jack switched on the recorder. 'Tammy I want to ask you a number of questions about Carrie Jefferies so I can build up a picture about her and about what happened last Sunday. Are you okay with that?'

Tammy nodded pulling her cardboard cup towards her.

'First of all tell me a little about Carrie. I know you said you didn't know much about her, but you obviously know some things, so just give us what you can. Tell me a little about her character, what you know about her, where she comes from etcetera.'

She wrapped her hands around her coffee cup but didn't pick it up. She set her eyes upon the wishy-washy liquid surface and without looking up said, 'It's like you've just said, I don't know that much about Carrie. We've only talked to one another on a dozen, or so, occasions in the two and a half years she and Toby have been down here. It's Toby I know more about. Well I say I know more about. I only know about him because of my husband James. Like I said earlier he's an artist like Toby. They met at an exhibition in London a couple of years ago and when James introduced himself, and told him where he lived, Toby said he'd just inherited his parents place overlooking Merthen Point, which is not far from us. He told James he'd turned one of the rooms into his studio and he invited him to visit. James went a couple of times to his house and then he invited Toby back to our house for a meal and that's how I met him and Carrie.' She rolled the cup back and forth, her eyes firmly fixed on the coffee's now rippling surface. 'To be honest the first time we met I took an instant dislike to him. He was so arrogant, so cock-sure of himself, going on about everything he'd achieved as an artist. I mean he is a good artist, there's no denying that. His paintings are beautiful, but it just grated on me. James and I are not that kind of people so whenever he came around, if it wasn't for a meal, I used to leave James and him to it. To be fair Toby has helped James a little. He's introduced him to a couple of the galleries he exhibits at in London.' She lifted her eyes, 'James gets on well with him but I'm afraid I didn't see beyond his big-headedness. I got on better with Carrie.' She took a deep breath and her tenseness slackened. 'Carrie was completely different to Toby – she was nice. 'Her mouth broke into a thin smile. 'By that I mean she was so easy to get on with. And she had this gorgeous Australian accent. The first night I met her she came into the kitchen while I was preparing the food. She'd left James and Toby talking in the lounge and asked me if she could have another glass of wine. We just got chatting and she said something about how 'up-their-arses' the pair were about their art. That broke the ice and we just got on after that. She asked me how I'd met James and then told me she'd met Toby at an exhibition she'd attended in London and he'd introduced himself by asking if he could paint her.'

'That's a different chat up line,' interrupted Fabi.

Tammy shared a smile with her. 'It may have been, but Toby is what they call a figurative painter, and Carrie does have a lovely figure and striking features and I think at the time it was an approach which was nothing more than that he wanted to paint her. Anyway, she told me she sat for him a couple of times, and she said that the paintings were really good and went down well at the gallery where he exhibits, and so she sat for him some more, and after six months they ended up in a relationship. She did share with me, when we talked that first time, that, like me, she thought that Toby was a bit full-on and cocky, but that as she'd got to know him more she'd since seen a different side to him.'

Jack interceded, 'Did Carrie tell you any more about herself? You said she had an Australian accent. Was she Australian?'

'She said she was from a place in New South Wales and that she was supposedly on a tour of Europe, but that had changed since she'd met Toby and she didn't know what was next for her. Well anyway, during that first meal, James and Toby got wrapped up in their art again and Carrie and I just got talking about all kinds of things. She made a comment about how beautiful the cove where we lived was and asked me how long we'd lived here. Then that led on to her telling me that there were some equally beautiful sights in Australia but that everything was so far away, compared to how everything seemed so close together in this country. We got on to talk about Toby's house – she introduced it. She said she loved how it overlooked Merthen Point and how she loved walking down to the cove, and she hinted that she'd more than likely stay a bit longer, depending how things went with him.' She paused and glanced at Jack and Fabi. 'That's it I'm afraid in terms of her background. They've both been quite a few times to our house since and we've been a couple of times up to their place. Carrie's a wonderful cook, she puts me to shame.'

'What about the time Toby got drunk? You said he picked on Carrie. You also said she made a comment to you about her "being used to it". Did you witness any other times when he was verbally abusive to her?'

She fixed Jack's stare. 'I have done a couple of times. Toby liked a drink, and at the end of most of our evening's he was always the worse for wear, but generally he was good natured. Some of the nights have been really good fun and we've had some really good laughs together. But this past year I've seen a different side to him. By the end of some of our recent times together he's started having a dig at Carrie – picking on her for no reason. You could tell she didn't like it but she tried to dismiss it. She had this nervous laugh and she'd try to shrug it off, telling us that he didn't mean any harm, and that he'd regret what he said the next day and be apologising to her. But I'm afraid, me being me, I've stuck up for her a couple of times recently and that's made him worse.'

'When you say worse?'

'I don't mean violent, as in hitting her or anything, but he'd get really nasty with her.'

'By nasty, what do you mean?'

'It was nearly always to do with his art. He'd go on like he did, about how good he was and how much he was selling his paintings for, and she'd end up looking across at me and giving an exaggerated yawn, which I'd laugh at. A couple of times when he'd gone on too long she'd say something like, "can we change the subject" and he just flipped. He'd start shouting, calling her stupid, telling her that she knew nothing about art.' Pausing, she pushed away her untouched coffee before continuing, 'That's what started it on Saturday evening – talking about his painting. She said something about being fed up with all the sitting and posing for hours on end, and he reacted by saying something like, "You'd be nothing if it wasn't for me. No one would know you or even take a second look at you. I make you look beautiful you silly cow." I couldn't believe it. I just felt I needed to say something in her defence. I told him she was beautiful no matter how well he painted his picture and he just snapped back at me and asked me what I knew about beauty in a woman – was I a dyke.' Tammy bounced her gaze from Jack to Fabi. 'I was livid. I told him he was drunk and that I thought it was time for him to leave. He just got up and said he'd had enough of our company anyway and that we should be grateful. If it wasn't for him James wouldn't have got the galleries in London.' She clenched her hands and tightened her mouth. 'That was it, I told him he was a fucking piss-head and to fuck off. I've not sworn like that for years but he just got to me.'

Fabi let out a sharp laugh and it lightened the tension in Tammy. She let out a short laugh herself. 'They left after that. As I say, James helped Toby into his car and Carrie drove off.'

'And you've not seen or heard from Carrie since?'

Tight-lipped Tammy shook her head. 'As I said, I've left Carrie a couple of voicemails on her mobile but she's not come back to me, and the last time I rang her phone two days ago it went straight to voicemail which makes me think her phone is dead.'

'And what about Toby? You said earlier that he'd rung you to see if you'd heard from her?'

'Yes he's rung a couple of times. I answered the phone once, but I didn't want to talk to him so passed the phone to James and he's spoken with him. I know at first James said he thought that Carrie was just giving Toby a taste of his own medicine, but when we've talked about it I can see that James is just as concerned as me. He thinks something bad might have happened to Carrie as well.'

8

In the front passenger seat of the CID car, Fabi Nosenzo flipped open her faux leather work folder across her lap and started skip-reading the front sheet of the Missing Persons Aide Memoir, reminding herself of its content. She had completed many of these forms over the past four years, the majority of them being for teenagers who had run away for a couple of days – usually because of something that had happened in their lives. On each occasion those teenagers had returned none the worse for wear, unconcerned about the angst they had caused their family or carers. When she had sat down with them to discuss their disappearance and gone through things in detail, the conclusion had generally been that in the grand scheme of things the reason and nature for their departure had been pretty insignificant. However, this one featuring Carrie Jefferies was different. Her disappearance had an element of mystery behind it, especially that there was the possibility of a foul deed being done. This case gave her goose-bumps.

She looked up from the page and glanced at the road ahead to check where they were. They were travelling steadily along the winding B3315 and she had time to take in the features they were passing. She recognised that they were passing through the hamlet of Sheffield. She turned to her mentor Jack. He had one hand on the steering wheel whilst the other gripped the gearstick. He was staring out through the windscreen but she had the feeling from his studious look that his thoughts were elsewhere. She wondered, if like her, he was thinking about their forthcoming visit to Toby Alexander's house.

She said, 'What do you think then?'

Without taking his eyes off the road Jack responded, 'What do I think of what?'

'About this job?'

In a steady voice he answered, 'I have to say, from that chat with Tammy Callaghan I'm suspicious Fabi. The fact that this Toby

Alexander fellow we're going to see had a blazing row with his girlfriend five days ago, while in a drunken stupor, and that no one's heard from her since makes me very concerned. Very concerned indeed.'

'Are we going to bring him in?'

'We're going to have a little talk first and see what he has to say about things and just check if he's spoken with her during these last five days. And we'll also do a search of his place and see what we come up with. See if there's anything untoward.'

Fabi studied his face again. He was still staring out through the windscreen – his striking blue eyes fixed on the road ahead. Suddenly, for no apparent reason, some of the conversation she had overheard between Jack and the Detective Inspector that morning jumped inside her head prompting her to query, 'Do you mind if I ask you something?'

Keeping his gaze still ahead he answered, 'If its money you're after I'm skint.'

She grinned. 'No it's not money. It's about something the gaffer said to you this morning.'

His eyebrows knitted together, 'What was that then?'

'He said to you "welcome back to the fold." When I got my placement for CID, and they told me I was coming to Penzance, and that you were going to be my mentor, I asked a few of my colleagues about you and I got the impression that you were almost a fixture in CID…'

'Fixture!' he cried, darting her a quick glance.

'Sorry Jack I didn't mean it like that. Those are my words not theirs. What some of them actually said, was that you were a steady guy, that you'd been in CID a long time at Penzance and that you were well thought of and a great detective.'

'You recovered well there Fabi. You'll make a good CID officer yet.'

'That's the truth Jack. The people I talked with made nice comments about you. They said I couldn't wish to work with anyone better.'

'That's alright then. As long as I'm not regarded as a fixture.'

Crestfallen she replied, 'I'm sorry Jack. I didn't mean it like that. I feel awful now. Have I got off on the wrong foot?'

The corners of his mouth turned up, 'I'm playing with you Fabi. I am a steady guy. I know that, and yes I have been at Penzance a long time, but that's to my advantage. I know all the villains there and I know what they're up to. There's very little of what goes on in that place gets past me.'

Fabi caught the intensity and sharpness in his eyes as he dashed across a look. She issued an apologetic smile. 'You forgive me then?'

'You're forgiven.'

She heaved a sigh of relief, 'Good.' Then, following a few seconds pause she said, 'So just picking back up on what I was going to ask you before I got side-tracked. Just before the DI introduced me he welcomed you back. He made it sound as if you'd been away a while. Have you been off doing something else? Been on another job elsewhere?'

Without looking her way, he said, 'No, I've been off sick for a few months. I only came back ten days ago.'

As he answered Fabi explored his look. While his voice wavered and his reply was hurried his expression remained dead-pan and he never once diverted his glance like he had done a few seconds earlier. She read something in that which intrigued her, though the impression she got from his rejoinder told her she shouldn't take this conversation any further. For some strange reason she felt as though she had put her foot in it again and she dropped her gaze back to her Missing Persons Aide Memoir. And, while she wanted to ask him more, her sub-conscious was telling her not to probe any further. She decided to listen to it – at least for now.

9

Taking the next left after the signpost to Boskenna, they turned onto a single track road flanked by ancient flint and granite stone walls, which Jack carefully negotiated for several hundred metres until they came to a gateway where a black slate plaque scripted with fading white paint announced their arrival at 'Renaissance Cottage'. They entered a driveway covered with loose gravel, which sent up loud crunching noises no matter how slowly Jack drove.

There goes my surprise attack, he said to himself, screwing up his face. Seconds later he drew up outside a stone built cottage capped with moss covered slate. The front door was protected by an elaborately carved Victorian wooden porch painted white. He mused that the place certainly had an element of charm. As he stepped out of the car the front door opened and a man stepped into the Victorian porch. For a moment he appeared to be watching them through the small window panes, unmoving, and then in one quick movement he snatched open the porch door and strode out onto the driveway.

Jack found himself faced by a slim, mid-thirties male, with dark, glistening, collar length, unruly hair, and a weather-beaten tanned complexion, who reminded him of the actor who played Ross Poldark in the TV series. He hadn't visualised Toby Alexander as being such a good looking man and, unexpectedly, it brought back a memory of him and his wife watching the series, picking out the locations they knew well; in particular, the coastal path from Botallack to Levant where the mining scenes had been filmed. It had been a regular walk of theirs when they had first met: When Claire had been healthy. Quickly dismissing the reminiscence, and recovering, he enquired, 'Toby Alexander?'

'Can I help you?' the voice was challenging.

Jack whipped out his warrant card from his inside coat pocket, held it up and introduced himself and Fabi, adding, 'We're from Penzance CID.'

Toby bounced his gaze from one detective to the other. 'Is this about Carrie?'

Poker-face Jack replied, 'Yes we're here about Carrie Jefferies, Mr Alexander.'

'Have you found her?'

'Can we come in please?' Though the words were not forceful Jack's actions were. Finishing his sentence, he swelled his chest and marched forward.

Toby Alexander moved to one side letting Jack brush past him.

Fabi followed into the oak-panelled hallway and Toby closed the door behind them. 'Shall we go into the lounge?' Toby said, extending an arm.

The room Jack and Fabi were shown into appeared dull and drab and smelt fusty. Heavy drapes covering the window hadn't been fully opened, and the furnishings were dark wood and leather, adding to the dowdiness of the surroundings. Jack quickly scanned the room. The furniture was jaded but he knew it was antique; a writing bureau and an upright glass fronted book case crammed with old books that he identified as Georgian, and although not currently fashionable he guessed they must have cost the owner a packet. As he took another look around he couldn't help but think how dreary and unfashionable the surroundings were, especially given how relatively young Toby Alexander was, and then he remembered Tammy Callaghan telling them that Toby had inherited the house from his parents and instantly the visual aspect made sense. Shifting his gaze to the open fire, straight away he was drawn to a large painting hanging above the mantelpiece. The picture was of an auburn, long-haired woman wearing a black silk kimono, standing by a set of French windows, bathed in warm sunlight. Her head was half-turned looking out into the garden, as if captivated by something she had seen or was just day-dreaming. Though the features weren't clear because of the loose painting style, Jack couldn't help but think that, in a mysterious way, she looked stunning. He found himself roaming his eye around the canvas. The painting and its subject had grabbed him.

'That's Carrie.'

Jack pulled back his gape and met Toby Alexander's studious look.

Toby nodded back to the painting. 'That's my favourite of Carrie. It was the first one I did of her. I decided to keep it instead of putting it in the gallery.' His eyes seemed to linger over it for a couple of seconds as if lost in thought. Then, dragging back his gaze he turned to the wall opposite.

Jack followed his look to where another six paintings hung. They were all figurative, and appeared to be of the same auburn-haired woman, in one of them she was nude, although she was elegantly portrayed reclining on a green velvet chaise lounge.

Toby continued, 'Those are also my favourite of her.'

Jack gave each of these paintings the once-over, though he didn't labour his eyes over any one of them like he had the one above the fireplace. Returning to Toby he muttered, 'Very nice.'

Toby gave a half-smile and offered them the large Chesterfield sofa in front of the window overlooking the drive. He dumped himself down in a button-leather high-backed chair next to the fireplace, facing them.

Jack lowered himself onto the sofa but unexpectedly found himself sinking with the cushions, and he quickly shuffled sideways to the arm where he found the springs more supportive. He re-arranged his jacket and made himself comfortable.

Fabi set herself down close to the other arm. She opened up her folder and unclasped her pen.

Toby looked from one detective to the other. 'Do you mind me asking? Who told you about Carrie?'

'Told us what Mr Alexander?'

'That she's gone missing. I'm presuming that's why you're here?' Then his face morphed into a look of concern. 'Nothing's happened to her has it?'

'Jack shook his head, 'We're here because someone expressed their concern about her.'

'Tammy. It's Tammy isn't it?' he exclaimed with an edge of annoyance in his voice.

Keeping a straight face Jack responded, 'Mrs Callaghan has reported to us that she has tried to make contact with Carrie over the past couple of days, but has been unable to do so. Therefore, she is concerned as to her whereabouts. Gathering by what you have just said I'm presuming she is missing and, if that is the case, then Mrs Gallagher has every right to be concerned and contact us.'

Toby huffed, 'I didn't mean it to come out like that. Course she has a right to be concerned, but I don't think Carrie is missing as in "missing persons contact the police" sort of missing.'

'Well how do you define the meaning of her being missing?'

'We had an argument. She got mad with me and drove off, and now she's making me stew on things for a couple of days before she comes back. You'll see.'

'Have you been in touch with her then?'

'No. She's not answering her phone.'

'So how do you know she'll be back?'

Toby seemed to think on the question, all the time his mouth setting tighter and tighter. After several seconds of silence, he answered, 'I don't. I'm just hoping she will. She's not taken anything with her. Her clothes are still in the wardrobe.'

'When did she go missing?'

'Last Sunday. Early hours, I think.' He shrugged his shoulders.

'You didn't see her go then?'

He shook his head. 'To be honest I'd had a good drink. We had an argument and when I woke up in the morning she'd gone. Taken her car. I tried ringing her but she wouldn't answer. I left her a couple of messages but now I can't get through at all. Her phone's not even going to voicemail. It's just dead.'

10

'Did you have a fight Mr Alexander?' asked Jack.

'How do you mean fight?'

'As in the physical sense. Did you come to blows?'

There was a split-second pause and then Toby answered, 'No. We just rowed.'

Jack caught a brief flicker of Toby's eyelids just before he answered. It was hardly noticeable but his years of experience told him it was something he should register. He mentally stored it and said, 'What was your argument about Mr Alexander?'

His mouth pursed, 'It was nothing really.'

'Well Mrs Callaghan didn't think it was nothing. She told us that you started it and that throughout the evening you had frequent digs at Carrie.'

Toby started fidgeting in his chair. 'If you want to know things have been little fractious between us just lately. Carrie knows exactly what buttons to push to fire me up. She had a go at me about my art and I just snapped.'

Jack thought about Toby's answer. Tammy Callaghan's version of events had been different but he decided not to develop anything at the moment. He said, 'When you say things have been fractious between you lately, what do you mean?'

'Just that things have been a bit rocky of late between us.' He let out an exasperated sigh, 'Look, I make my living from art, especially painting the female form. The bank crash in two-thousand-and-eight was devastating for artists like me and it's been a slow recovery ever since. It's put a strain on things and I guess it's got to me at times. When Carrie has a go at my art she's having a go at the way I make my living. I know I shouldn't react like I do, but I do. And Saturday night I'd had a drink. Probably too much to drink. I know it's my fault we argued.'

Jack watched Toby's face take on a look of mild-embarrassment. Nodding slowly, he said, 'So you had an argument at Mr and Mrs Callaghan's place and then Carrie drove you home. Did you argue in the car?'

Toby glanced up to the ceiling, studying the question. Then, returning his gaze he replied, 'No, I don't think so. I think I must have dropped off on the way home. To be honest I can just remember James helping me into the car and I can't remember much else.'

'What about when you got home?'

'I said I don't remember anything. When I woke up the next day Carrie had taken the car and gone.'

Jack again thought there was something worth registering about Toby's look as he answered. Pushing himself forward he said, 'Do you think she's run away then Mr Alexander?'

'I think that's what she's done. I think in a couple of days' time she'll be back.'

'Is there anyone she's likely to be staying with?'

'Carrie's from Australia. She hardly knows anyone here. The people she knows are the people I know, so I don't think so. The only place I can think she'd likely to go to is James and Tammy's and I've already spoken to them.'

'Okay, we'll need to take down a few details.'

'Why? Do you think something's happened to her?'

Jack threw him a phoney smile, 'This is just procedure Mr Alexander – so we can circulate her details.' Maintaining the sham pretence, he added, 'Is Carrie Jefferies her full name?'

Looking thoughtful Toby nodded, 'I'm saying it is, but to be honest I don't know if she has any other names beside Carrie. I haven't actually seen anything with her name on. We met eighteen months ago and we've been together just under twelve months. She modelled for me after we met at one of my exhibitions and we just hit it off. As I say Carrie's from Australia. When we first met in London she told me she'd been made redundant from her job back home and was using some of the money to tour Europe which she'd always wanted to do.'

'And whereabouts in Australia was home for Carrie?'

'The exact place?' He offered up a surprised look, 'Do you know, again, I don't actually know. She told me she came from New South Wales. Like I say, I've never seen anything with her name or address on it and I've never thought to ask her.'

'Not seen her passport then?'

Toby seemed to think about the question for a few seconds then answered, 'No I don't recall seeing it. As far as I remember she's never needed to prove who she is and I've never gone through her things.'

'What about her family? Her friends?'

'As far as I know she had no family. She told me her parents were dead and she's never mentioned having brothers or sisters. I know she's never been married.' He paused before continuing, 'Or at least that's what she told me and I've no reason not to believe her. As to her friends, I can't recall any names. I've heard her chatting on her mobile quite a few times and afterwards she's told me it's either one of her mates, or an ex-colleague who's been asking after her, but as to any names I'm afraid not.'

'Okay Mr Alexander no problems we'll make a few phone calls. She'll have had to register with the Border Agency when she came into the country. We'll be able to get some information from her passport details to give us a starting point.' Jack glanced across to Fabi who was busy making notes. He brought back his look to Toby, 'Now you say she took her car?'

'It's actually my car. I bought it for her to use. It's a mini. I've got the registration documents in a drawer in the kitchen.'

'Good. We'll be able to put a marker on it on the Police National Computer and then we can track it down the minute it uses a major road.'

Toby acknowledged with a nod.

'What was she wearing the last time you saw her – Sunday wasn't it you said?'

'Well it was just after midnight on Saturday when we left James and Tammy's so it would have been about half twelve when we got back here. As I say I can't remember anything after that, but that night she went out dressed in a black and white striped jumper and a pair of black skinny jeans.'

'Now what about a photograph of her so we can circulate what she looks like?'

Toby stroked his chin and gave back a considered look. Shaking his head, he replied, 'I don't have any of her.'

Jack screwed up his face, 'Not one?'

Toby shook his head again, 'Nope.'

'Not even on your phone?'

'No.'

Jack pointed to the large painting above the wall. 'Didn't you take any of her when you were painting her?'

'No I've painted every picture of her from life. She'd pose for me for a couple of hours at a time. We'd do the paintings over several sessions and I'd finish them in my studio – put in bits of light effect here and there to give the painting its zing.'

'What about social media.'

'As far as I know she never used it. The only time she went on the computer was to do some online shopping.'

Jack took another look at the paintings and quickly determined that none of them had enough detail in the face to enable their use in a missing person's circulation. An idea popped into his head. 'What about her driving licence or her passport?'

'She'll have her driving licence with her in her bag. I don't know where her passport is. I think she carries that around with her.'

'You say you've tried ringing her mobile?'

Toby nodded. 'Yes, but like I say she's either turned it off or it's dead.'

'Have you got her number?'

Toby reached into his pocket and pulled out his mobile. Searching his contacts, he brought up Carrie's mobile number and showed it to Fabi. She copied the number onto her report.

'We'll be able to do a location search now we've got this. We should be able to find her.'

Toby's expression signified hopefulness.

Jack pushed himself up from the sofa. 'We've got everything we can get for now Mr Alexander. There's just one more thing we need to do before we leave you in peace, and again, this is just procedure. We need to do a quick search of the place, just for my own piece of mind.' The grin Jack shot Toby was once again false. Intended to make Toby think that he shouldn't be worried about anything, but hidden behind Jack's smile was suspicion, and as he straightened and took another look at Carrie's portrait above the fire he couldn't help but think that things were not quite right.

11

Jack and Fabi sat in the CID car watching Toby Alexander close the porch door.

'Not much to go on,' said Fabi staring out through the windscreen.

Toby Alexander remained in the porch, watching them.

Jack played with his bottom lip, 'I'm not happy about this one bit. There were a few times when I was questioning him I caught a hesitancy before he answered. I can't put my finger on what it was but mark my words there's something not right here.' He turned over the engine, revved gently and pulled away slowly. As he coasted down the drive he looked back through his rear view mirror, Toby was still there, watching. He continued, 'There's no sign in that house that she made any preparations to leave. Her clothing's all there. Her toothbrush is still in the bathroom and most importantly all her lotions and make up are still on the dressing table. You tell me what woman would do a runner without their makeup.'

'Ooh Jack Buchan, you sexist.' Fabi grinned to show him she was only joking.

'Something I was taught at detective training school – look at everything, leave nothing unturned, challenge everything, and it's always stayed with me and that's why I say that.'

'What next then?'

'We need to find out who else knows her, beside Toby and the Callaghans. We'll speak to Tammy again and see if she can help. We'll also get the car circulated, see if we can get any sightings of it. And, we need to e-mail the techie people and feed them her mobile number and see if they can get a location of it for us. Finally, for now, we make some enquiries with The Border Agency and just check she's not left the country. Though, my guess is she won't have, so we'll also see what information they've got on her which will help fill in the gaps.'

'Back to the station then?'

Turning out of the driveway onto the single track road Jack replied, 'After a little diversion. I need to let my dog out into the garden because you and I will not be home on time today. We've got quite a bit of work ahead of us.'

***

On the way back to Penzance Jack pulled off the narrow winding road and followed the sign to Mousehole, where, on entering the village of Paul, he deviated right off the main street and into a side road, reducing his speed as he pulled towards the kerb. As the offside tyres scraped the edge of the pavement he braked, set the handbrake and turned off the engine.

Fabi eyed the front of the detached stone cottage they had stopped outside, with its original wooden windows and white four-panelled door. 'This yours?' she asked.

'My humble abode,' he replied getting out of the car.

'Beautiful,' she responded following him onto the footpath.

Inserting the key in the lock Jack called back over his shoulder, 'Don't mind dogs do you Fabi?'

'I love dogs. We had one when I was a kid. A golden lab – Honey. She died when I was fourteen. I think about her from time to time and I'd love to have another dog but my lifestyle wouldn't be fair on it.'

He turned the key and pushed open the front door. Instantly a brown and white Springer Spaniel darted through the gap launching itself at its master's legs. Jack bent down, ruffled its neck fur, shepherding the dog backwards into the hall while still fussing it. 'Meet Mollie' he said without looking up. As soon as Fabi stepped over the threshold the dog turned its attention to her, targeting her with its big brown eyes, feverishly wagging its tail.

'My, you're a cutie,' Fabi said, fondling the Springer's ears as it brushed against her.

'She'll have you doing that all day,' Jack half-laughed. 'I'll let her out in the garden and stick the kettle on. You make yourself comfortable.' He chinned towards a room on the left and pulled Mollie away from his colleague. 'Come on girl,' he called heading to the kitchen.

As the Springer scampered away Fabi pushed open the door and stepped into a small, but bright and inviting lounge. It had a low beamed ceiling, polished wooden floor, partially covered by a floral pattern rug, cream plaster walls and a feature log burner set in an open hearth. It was simply furnished with two, two-seater sofas set around a light oak coffee table, which she couldn't help but notice was untidily littered with an array of photographs and magazines. More photographs were scattered across the cushions of one of the sofas. Intrigued, she picked up a handful and began leafing through them. In almost every photo a much younger Jack was posing with an attractive brunette. She diverted her gaze and viewed several of the other photographs on the coffee table. These were similar in nature – Jack with the pretty brunette, but in different settings and in different locations. A lot of them appeared to be holiday snaps. Jack looked to be between his late twenties to late thirties, and she couldn't help smiling to herself as she ran her eyes over them. His sandy coloured hair hadn't changed much, especially its wavy, collar-length, untidy looking style, though a little grey had crept into the temples since these had been taken. And he had put on some weight. Looking at one of a beach location, in which she guessed he was early thirties, Jack was well toned, with a flat stomach. Now he was a lot broader and his stomach had developed a slight paunch. The sparkle in his intense blue eyes hadn't changed though. She was just thinking to herself 'quite a handsome man in your time' when the door opened and in trotted Mollie followed by Jack holding out two steaming mugs. Still clasping the handful of photographs, she couldn't stop herself blushing – as if she'd been caught out doing something she shouldn't be doing. She responded, 'I was just looking through your photo's – I hope you don't mind?'

Jack's face took on a perturbed look, though it didn't last long, as he broke into a half-smile and said, 'Course not. Just a few distant memories.' Then, presenting her with a mug, he added, 'It's coffee?'

'Coffee's good.' Fabi placed the photographs back on the table and took the mug from Jack's grasp.

He offered Fabi the tidy sofa, while he dropped down on the one containing the scattered photographs, brushing them aside as he made himself comfortable.

'She's very pretty,' said Fabi tipping her head at the photos. 'Your wife?'

'Was my wife – Claire – she died just over six months ago.'

'Oh I'm sorry Jack.'

He shrugged his shoulders, 'One of those things.'

She sipped at her coffee without taking her eyes from his, 'I don't mean to pry, but is that why you were off sick? What we were talking about earlier?'

He gave her a thoughtful look, took a drink and then answered, 'Look it's no secret. You'll find out anyway sooner or later.' He paused a moment before continuing, 'Claire committed suicide. I came home late one evening last September and found her in the bath. She'd taken an overdose and cut her wrists.'

'Gosh, I'm really sorry...' Taking a pause herself she studied his face, then said, 'You don't need to say anymore Jack.'

'No, it's okay, I'm fine. I'm through the worst.' He drew in a breath and continued, 'Claire was depressed. Had been depressed a long time.' He paused and glanced up to the ceiling before returning his gaze. 'She had her good days and her bad days. It had been going on for years. The sad thing is I actually thought she was coming through the worst of it. Then I came home that night and found her. She certainly hadn't messed about.'

'Wow Jack, Some shocker.'

'It was, believe me. The sad thing though is she never rang me or anything that day. Not that she normally did, but I just keep thinking if only she had I might have been able to do something. She never even left a note.' He took another drink of his coffee, glimpsed down at the photographs and said, 'I'll never know what came over her. What made her do that?' Then, pulling himself back from his trance added, 'No use being maudlin over it. Got to move on. Got a job to do eh?' He fixed Fabi's eyes. 'You and I have got a missing woman to find.'

12

'What have you got then Jack?' asked Detective Inspector Dick Harrison looking over the DC's shoulder. In his mid-forties, The DI was a tall gangly man with short brown naturally spiky hair.

Jack looked up from his computer screen and fixed his boss's grey eyes. Twenty years ago Dick Harrison had been another junior detective he had tutored. And, like many entering the department he had witnessed that enthusiasm and competitive edge that had made him an ideal candidate for CID. But he also saw in Dick ambition. Ambition, which Dick had shared with him on many occasion and which he had encouraged. Since then Dick had gained promotion – first to Sergeant and then Inspector, and three years ago he had returned to Penzance as the departments DI, rekindling their working relationship and their friendship. Jack answered, 'Strange one Dick.' He only ever called him by his first name when there was no one else in the office.

'Genuinely missing?'

'Can't work it out. She's taken her car and mobile, and it looks as though she's also taken her bank and credit cards, and her passport – she's Australian – and on that basis I would have said she'd just had enough of an abusive man and done a runner. But then she's left behind all her clothes and make-up and toiletries and I ask myself why.'

'How long has she been missing?'

'Six days now.'

'And no one's heard from her?'

Jack shook his head. 'Nope. Not a dickie-bird since Sunday. We've tried her mobile number and the phone is dead. Fabi's nipped over to headquarters to have a personal word with the techies to see if we can speed up a trace. And I've entered the car on ANPR to see if we can get a hit on it.' ANPR is the automatic number place recognition system, used by the police and security services to track vehicles. The UK's road network CCTV cameras were linked to a main computer, and Jack knew that if Carrie travelled in her car on any of the major roads they would get instant notification.

'Do we have any idea where she's likely to go if she has simply upped sticks and gone?'

Jack gave a gentle shake of his head, 'As I said she's Australian. According to Toby her friends and contacts are all over there. As far as we know the only people she knows here are her boyfriend and the Callaghans.'

'Could she be having an affair? Especially, I'm thinking, if things have not been going too well between her and Toby.'

'That's an avenue I'm going to explore. I'm going to have another word with Tammy Callaghan and I'm going to speak with the owner of the gallery in London where Toby exhibits.'

'And what about this Toby fellow? Anything known about him?'

'Well according to Tammy he has a nasty temper when he's drunk, but only in a verbal way. She's never seen Toby assault Carrie and Carrie's never hinted or said he has to her. And, I've checked him out on PNC – there's no record of him.'

'So what next then Jack? Do we run an incident?'

'Just hang fire until I've got the results back from her mobile, and the ANPR check, and I've also got an enquiry being done by the Border Agency, just in case she's gone back to Australia. If those all come back negative then I'll come back to you and we'll look at the next steps.'

The DI rested a hand on Jack's shoulder, 'Okay your call. Keep me in the loop. The minute you think we need to ratchet this up you let me know.'

13

Toby Alexander was restless. He was standing in front of the dining room French doors looking out over his bleak garden and across the fields in the direction of the sea, unable to concentrate because his thoughts were leaden. Suddenly his ears picked up to the sound of the six o'clock news starting in the next room, and with images of Carrie still tumbling around inside his head he dragged away his gaze and trundled toward the lounge. Standing before the TV he listened to the female newscaster going through the day's headlines and then followed the brief switch across to the local TV where he listened to those leading bulletins. When he heard there was nothing on about Carrie he let out a heavy groan and pulled away his eyes, switching them to her portrait hanging above the fire. Toby thought he knew Carrie pretty well, but since the police had left he realised he actually knew very little about her at all. He had tried his best to answer every question they had fired at him but he could tell by the looks on their faces that they were suspicious. Especially the man – what was his name – DC Buchan. He was certain the detective had caught the tentativeness in his voice when he'd responded to his enquiry as to whether he and Carrie had fought. The thing was, as soon as he'd asked the question the image of the broken glass and bloodstained kitchen floor had flash-banged inside his head messing up his thinking.

Suddenly overcome with frustration he balled his hands into fists, threw back his head and screamed 'Fuck' to the ceiling. He held his head there for a few seconds before returning his eyes to the portrait. 'Where the hell are you Carrie?' Settling his gaze on her painted face he pondered on the question, the mental picture of the mess on his kitchen floor re-entering his brain. Had something happened to her? Had he done something to her? The answer to both those questions was – he wasn't sure.

***

Toby awoke with a start, his mind going into tail-spin. He thought he had heard a cry – it might have even been a scream. He lay in his bed, holding his breath, exploring the bedroom and straining his ears. He had not closed the curtains again, and moonlight washed in through the window creating scary images within the shadows, firing up his imagination. For a few seconds he thought that one of those apparitions in the ghostly half-light was Carrie's face, horribly disfigured and he felt the hairs on the back of his neck bristle. Rubbing his eyes, he started to turn away, and as he did so a sharp cracking noise, sounding like a stone hitting the window, made him jump. He froze. A couple of seconds later another chink resounded. In one swift movement he threw back the duvet and jumped out of bed. In two strides he was at the window, staring out, trying to pierce the night's darkness. Adjusting his sight, he scanned quickly around his garden. By the Sycamore, in the left-hand corner, his gaze halted. He thought he caught movement. It was only a Will-O'-the-Wisp type of movement, but it grabbed his attention. He probed the shadows thrown by the trunk and there he saw a shape... a silhouette and it appeared to be human. Screwing up his eyes, he explored further. Someone in dark clothing, their outline limned in moon-glow, was staring up at his window. Staring up at him... and he was naked. Suddenly, he felt vulnerable and he stepped sharply back from the window, retreating into shadow. As he did so his bedside phone rang. His heart almost leapt from his chest. It took him a couple of seconds to snatch his breath, and then, taking another stride, he seized the receiver in mid-ring, hit the answer button and held it to his ear. At first he didn't say anything. He just listened, trying to calm his racing heartbeat. No one spoke to him, though he thought he caught the sound of someone breathing. It was soft, yet ragged. After ten seconds of not getting a response, with some trepidation, he said 'Hello?'

Following a moments silence a throaty voice hissed, 'I know you killed her!'

14

The London art gallery where Toby Alexander exhibited was on the Kings Road in Chelsea. Jack and Fabi travelled by train from Penzance into Paddington and then caught the tube across London to South Kensington where they emerged onto a bustling Kings Road. The gallery's, swish double fronted premises, was just a short walk from the Underground.

Before entering the building, Jack stopped by one of the display windows and eyed a couple of the paintings on show, whistling through his teeth as he took in some of the price tags. Half turning, he said to Fabi on a low note, 'These would cost me half my year's wages.'

'Some people have got more money than sense,' Fabi replied. 'If I had that type of money to spend on something, it wouldn't be a painting. It would be a five-star holiday in the Maldives with my partner.'

'New car for me,' Jack grinned, 'I think art lovers would call us Philistines,' he added, pushing open the door.

The inside of the gallery was opulent, with white painted walls and ceilings, and was fitted out with high-end contemporary furnishings and thick pile rugs. Every bit of space was lit by overhead bright white spotlights, showing off the display of evenly spaced paintings adorning the walls.

Jack hadn't had time to close the door before a man, who looked to be in his early fifties, appeared. He was slim and tanned with silver grey hair and was dressed in a Harris Tweed jacket and dark jeans. Jack noticed he had on a pair of expensive looking tan brogues. He had always wanted a pair like them but had never been able to justify spending the £500 on a pair of shoes. The man showed off a perfect set of white teeth behind a fixed smile.

'Can I help you?' he greeted.

'We're here to speak with David Muir.' Jack replied.

'I'm David Muir.'

Jack took out his warrant card, showed it to the gallery owner and introduced Fabi and himself. 'We spoke with your secretary yesterday. We're here to ask you some questions about Mr Alexander, one of your artists.'

'Oh yes, Pippa mentioned it. He's not in any trouble is he?'

'It's not exactly him we are here about. It's his girlfriend we want to ask some questions about. She's gone missing and we want to talk to anyone who might know her.'

'Carrie?'

Jack and Fabi nodded in unison.

'You know her?' asked Jack.

The man nodded. 'Yes. Well, when I say yes, I know her as Toby's girlfriend.' Pausing he added, 'You say she's gone missing? What do you mean?'

'I'm afraid I can't go into all the details Mr Muir, but six days ago Carrie left the house she shared with Mr Alexander and she's not been seen or heard of since. We're trying to establish if she's been in touch with anyone in these last five days. We've been told she's Australian and knows very few people in this country, but we know she's been here a few times with Mr Alexander and we've been told she actually met him here at one of his exhibitions.'

'Yes that's right, his autumn two-thousand-and-twelve one. She came to the opening night. She took a real interest in his work and they got chatting. Quite a stunner is Carrie and Toby can be a bit of a charmer. He ended up asking her if he could paint her portrait. I don't know if you've seen any pictures of her but the paintings he's done of her are spectacular. She is a gorgeous subject and they certainly go down well with our clients. I'll show you some shall I?' David Muir pointed them down the gallery and set off, stopping at an alcove near the back, where, with a theatrical flick of his wrist, he presented four figurative paintings of a striking auburn haired woman. In two of the paintings she was draped across a bed, her hair radiating out against an emerald green satin sheet in very alluring poses.

Jack instantly saw the resemblance of the woman in these paintings to the ones he had viewed back in Toby Alexander's cottage. In fact, in one of them he noted she was wearing the same black kimono. Despite the lack of detail in the brushwork Carrie

Jefferies portraits had an almost erotic appeal, and once more he found himself transfixed by her painted image.

'You can see why Mathew wanted her as his model can't you?'

David Muir's comment broke Jack out of his reverie. 'Mathew?'

The gallery owner's mouth tightened. 'Sorry I slip up from time to time. Yes. Mathew. He now goes by Toby but his first name is Mathew. Mathew Tobias Alexander to be precise. He only became Toby after the tragedy.'

'Tragedy?'

David Muir cast his gaze from Jack to Fabi and back, 'Yes, his girlfriend Angel.' He paused a moment exchanging glances, as if waiting for a reaction. Then he said, 'You don't know about Angel?' Pausing again and searching out their faces he said, 'She committed suicide. That's why he changed his name. It caused him all kinds of problems.'

Jack fixed the gallery owners look, 'Is there somewhere private we can talk.'

15

Jack, Fabi and David Muir made themselves comfortable in dark-brown leather tub seats set around a glass top table in a back room. It also served as a kitchen area for making drinks. A pretty, fair-haired, slim woman, in her mid-twenties, dressed in a black and white 60s shift style dress, set down three cups of coffee in front of them.

David Muir said, 'This is Pippa. Pippa Johnson. She's my assistant.'

Jack met her eyes, 'My apologies Pippa. I thought you were the secretary when we spoke yesterday.'

She held his gaze for a good few seconds and presented a nervous smile. Then pushing a cup towards him, she turned away and left the room leaving the door ajar.

'Pippa has been with me almost five years now. She's the daughter of a good client of mine. I was introduced to her just after she had finished her art history degree. She wanted a job. Initially it was just so she could put something on her CV, but she's was such an absolute godsend that I persuaded her to stay.'

Jack acknowledged with a brief nod, glanced at his coffee and, deciding that it looked too hot to drink, returned to face David Muir. 'Before I ask you about Carrie tell me about Mr Alexander and this Angel.'

David picked up his cup and, clasping it between both hands, replied, 'Surely you must have heard about it. It was headline news. Angel was a well know fashion model.'

'Of course!' interjected Fabi slapping her thigh. 'I wondered where I'd heard that name before.' She looked from David to Jack, 'Angel May, she's been on the front of most fashion magazines at one time or another. And she had some make-up named after her. She died of a drugs overdose a few years ago didn't she? It was all over the news.'

'Five years ago.' David's mouth tightened. 'It was terrible. The inquest verdict was that it was accidental but some people blamed

Mathew for her death. Some even accused him of supplying the drugs she took. Rumours were that it was hard drugs she'd died from, but the post mortem revealed it was an overdose of anti-depressants.' He sipped at his coffee, then, removing the cup from his lips said, 'It wasn't Mathew who had anything to do with it of course, but the rumour-mill had done the damage. His painting suffered for a while and none of his work sold. Especially the paintings he had done of Angel, which was a shame, because they were just exquisite. Mathew was a very talented artist when I met him ten years ago and he began exhibiting with me, but it was the paintings of Angel that made him. When she died Mathew almost became a pariah overnight and so he decided it would be best if he changed his name and move away from London. He dropped his first name, shortened his middle name and took on a place in Cornwall, near where he used to live, and that kept him out of the limelight. Then when his Mother died in two-thousand-and-eleven, his father was already dead, he was left the family home and he made his studio there. It allowed him some breathing space and, as things quieted down, he painted some new pieces and we held the first exhibition of his new work, under his new name, in two-thousand-and-twelve. That time away had put some distance between him and what had happened and his exhibition wasn't far off a sell-out thank goodness. It put him back on the road and of course that's when he met Carrie.'

Jack made a quick note, recording the gist of what David Muir had just told him. It was something they could follow up on when they got back to Penzance. He said, 'What about that meeting between Mr Alexander and Carrie? Were you around?'

'Well, when you ask was I around, I was, but Mathew would do his thing working the room and I would do mine, encouraging people to buy – you know what I mean?'

Jack nodded. 'So you didn't witness their meeting?'

'Not as such. Mathew spoke to a lot of people, and it wasn't until later in the evening I saw him spending some time with Carrie. As I told you earlier, it didn't surprise me one bit when I saw him stuck to her side at the end of the night. I mean, she just stood out from the crowd – not just pretty but she had this aura about her. And of course, like I said, she was genuinely interested in his work. She hung around to the end, talking to Mathew and he introduced me to her. I chatted with her, but only briefly, because there were still a few clients around, but when we were closing up and there was only me and Mathew he told me he had invited her to pose for him. We had a bit of a joke about it because I knew that was how he got most of his women into bed, but he said Carrie was quite shy and it had taken him quite a bit of persuading to get her to pose for him.'

'And Mr Alexander started painting her?'

'Yes he did, but it wasn't until he brought a couple of new pieces into the gallery that I realised how serious he'd been about painting her. They were beautiful and I told him it was probably his best work. They were even better than the ones he'd done of Angel. That's when he told me that she'd moved in with him.'

'And this was?'

David Muir pondered on the question for a few seconds before answering, 'His exhibition was on October the fifth – Friday – that was when he met her, and then he brought in the new pieces of Carrie early in December, just before our Christmas exhibition.'

'Did you meet with Carrie again after that first meeting?'

'I got to meet her a couple of times when Mathew brought in more new work, and I did speak with her on the phone on a few occasions, but I didn't really get to know her as such. When she came to the gallery with Mathew he and I would talk business.'

'So you didn't know anything about her background?'

He shook his head, 'Other than that she was Australian and she told me she had taken six months out to tour Europe; no, I'm afraid not.'

'Okay David I think that's it.' Jack checked with Fabi, flashing a look, which said, 'is there anything you want to ask?' When she shook her head he took out one of his business cards and slid it across the table. 'If there's anything that comes to mind that's my number and email.'

16

Fabi picked up her bundle of papers, dragged out her chair and scooted it around the side of her desk to where Jack sat, and shuffled up next to him. Plonking down her paperwork she fanned it out across the desk, covering his workload.

She said, 'This is everything to do with the Angel May suicide. I've spent the best part of two and a half hours getting this lot. I've even managed to track down the detective who went to the job. He's told me some very interesting stuff.'

Jack gave her a sideways glance. 'Run me through it then and then I'll tell you what I've got.'

Fabi pulled out several sheets of computer generated newspaper articles and placed them before Jack. 'Angel May's real name was Angela Mayberry,' she flashed a quick look and added, 'That's something I've just learned.' She slid aside one of the digital reports headed by a photograph of a slender, very pretty, honey-blonde haired girl, wearing a tiny black bikini top only just managing to contain larger than average breasts. Jack picked up the picture and ran his eyes over it. Fabi chinned toward the A4 sheet and continued, 'She was often referred to by the nickname Barbie, because of her likeness to the doll, and it stuck – a bit like Twiggy. She was only twenty-three when she died. She was found dead in her apartment by her driver who'd come round to pick her up to take her to the airport. She should have been flying off to the Bahamas to do a swimwear photo-shoot for a catalogue.'

'When was this?'

Scrolling a finger down one of the sheets she halted on a line and replied, 'Friday 15th October, six years ago. It was just before nine in the morning when she was found. Her apartment was in Kensington. Not too far from the gallery where we went yesterday. She'd lived there just under two years.' She lifted her gaze. 'That's from the newspaper report, but then I've also got the run-down from the detective who investigated her death. First of all she wasn't popular with the other residents in her block. Too many wild parties apparently. She was a bit of a party-animal according to these reports.'

'Aren't they all? Young people with too much money to spend.'

Fabi threw him an exaggerated black-look, 'Now, now Jack, you were that age once.'

'I was married at that age and responsible.'

Fabi laughed and shook her head, 'Only because this job made you act like that. I'm sure given half the chance you'd have acted different.'

He smiled, 'Maybe so. Okay enough said about what I've missed out on. Tell me what the detective told you.'

'He told me that the driver let himself into her apartment, as was the norm apparently, and he found her on the floor beside her bed. He said he could tell she was dead by her face, but he still called the ambulance. A paramedic got there within four minutes of the call and confirmed that she was dead – had been for hours and he called the police. Uniform got there first and, finding her surrounded by pills, called in CID. When the detective got there, Angel's body was still in situ and he called in SOCO. There was nothing suspicious about the scene. The pills they found were her own anti-depressant tablets. Apparently she was on a regular prescription for depression, had been for roughly three months.' Fabi met Jack's gaze, 'Who'd have thought someone as beautiful and rich as her would be on anti-depressants. Just goes to show you eh?' Fabi shook her head and continued, 'Anyway her post mortem showed that, not only had she taken a substantial quantity of her anti-depressants, but there were also high levels of cocaine in her system. The detective said they found evidence of cocaine in her apartment, but only a small quantity, suggesting personal use only. This is where Mathew Alexander comes into the frame, and why he had such a bad time following her death.'

Jack's eyebrows knitted together.

Fabi looked at him and continued, 'A little background first. It's exactly as David Muir said yesterday – Mathew made his name from his paintings of Angel. He'd been painting her for about eighteen months and he'd had a number of sell-out exhibitions. You could say it was the perfect partnership – both promoting each other. The pair were also seen regularly out together around London and at various celebrity bashes. As you can probably imagine, because of the industry and the people she mixed with there were also lots of rumours flying around about her cocaine use. A couple of gossip magazines ran articles suggesting Angel's involvement but her agent always put out a rebuttal and blamed the hangers-on around her. However, once the media got hold of the info about cocaine being found in her system they had a field day, and Mathew was among many who had the finger pointed at them, but nothing was ever proved as to who exactly supplied her with the stuff. The detective told me he spoke with, and interviewed, a number of people including Mathew, but they either denied it or refused to say anything and so he never found out where the gear came from. As to her death, now this is where it gets interesting, and why Mathew had such a hard time after the inquest…' Fabi paused, studied Jack's probing look for a moment and then continued, 'The night before she was found dead Angel was seen with a group of people, including Mathew, in several pubs and bars around where she lived, and enquiries with neighbours revealed that shortly after midnight the sound of partying came from her apartment. One of the neighbours banged on her door about quarter-to-one and asked her to keep the noise down. It seemed she obliged for a while but around two a.m. a couple more neighbours reported that they were awoken to the sounds of arguing and things being thrown around inside Angel's apartment. The next door neighbour said he thought he heard Angel shouting and crying and called the police. Two officers attended, and Mathew tried door-stepping them, saying that Angel had gone to bed, but they persuaded him to let them in so that they could check that she was alright. When the officers went in Mathew was the only one around. He told the officers that there had been half a dozen people there earlier but as soon as the neighbour complained about the noise he thought it would be best that they leave. And so the only signs of partying were empty bottles and glasses. But they also reported that a vase was broken on the floor as well as a couple of photo frames and asked Mathew how that had happened. He told the officers that Angel had done it in a drunken temper and that she'd now gone to bed. Because of the mess, they insisted on seeing her and so he showed them into her bedroom. They found Angel partially undressed and in a bit of a state, both distressed and worse the wear for drink. She'd been crying but she refused to say anything other than that she was upset, and so after reassuring the officers she was okay they left.

The officers were asked if they thought she had been assaulted but they both insisted that there were no physical signs that she had been, and there were no signs of assault on her body following the pm. As to the broken vase and photo frames, at her inquest, a couple of her friends from the same modelling agency said that Angel was highly strung at times and was prone to the odd outburst – throwing things around. One of the girls also mentioned that on one occasion she had called round to Angel's apartment and found her having a go at Mathew, accusing him of shagging someone else. Who that person was, was never revealed, but when Mathew was challenged on that at the inquest he said that at times Angel could be insecure and would regularly accuse him of having sex, or an affair, with one person or another, for no reason. But apparently, his performance in the witness box wasn't that convincing. Not just about the allegations against him, but about the drug use, and the account he gave of the row he and Angel had had on the night prior to her death, and while the coroner didn't exactly accuse him of lying, he did question Mathew's directness and honesty over some of the things he had said when questioned. And, it was this that the press latched on to.'

'So the cocaine aspect was never bottomed? Where she'd got it from?'

'As I say, SOCO did find trace evidence of cocaine on the coffee table in Angel's apartment – but it was only a minute quantity. And tests on the table picked up Angel's and Mathews DNA and fingerprints. Mathew was interviewed under caution about this but his response was that it was Angel who had produced it that night, and he'd tried to prevent her from using it, and it was that which had sparked the argument and her outburst. The detective didn't believe Mathew one bit, but none of the witnesses at the party were forthcoming.'

'And what about after the police had left that night. What did Mathew get up to, because you haven't mentioned if he was at Angel's apartment when her driver or the Paramedic arrived?'

'He definitely wasn't there. CCTV in the foyer block picked him up leaving her place shortly after three-thirty a.m. which is about an hour after the police had left. He told the detective, that he'd cleaned up the mess, made sure Angel was okay and decided to go home and catch up with her the next day when she'd calmed down.'

'There were no indications that she was going to harm herself then?'

Fabi shrugged her shoulders, 'Mathew said not. He said if he'd thought for one minute she'd have done what she did he would have stayed.'

Jack rolled his eyes and clucked his tongue, 'He sounds all heart. I can see why he didn't come out of this very well'

'You and I both.'

'And what about her use of anti-depressants you said she'd been prescribed them?'

Fabi nodded, 'Three months prior to her death. The GP told the inquest that she'd visited his surgery on a couple of occasions complaining she was depressed and was having difficulty sleeping because her relationship with her boyfriend wasn't going well.'

With enquiring eyes Jack said, 'Boyfriend being Mathew?'

Fabi nodded, 'She wasn't seeing anyone else. Mathew was asked about this, but again he came up with a suitable answer that he thought that things were fine between them. He said he felt it was another sign of Angel's insecurity.'

Jack slowly shook his head, setting his mouth tight.

Picking up on his actions Fabi said, 'Neither the detective nor the coroner were too impressed with him but there was no hard evidence to knock what he said.'

'No evidence or suggestion that he assaulted Angel at any time?'

'None that the detective found during his enquiries. But he did say that the people he spoke to weren't the most helpful of witnesses. He always felt that they were either protecting themselves or the agency they and Angel worked for.'

'Usually the case.' Jack was quiet for a while, playing with his bottom lip. 'Anything else you've got? Angel's background? Family?'

'Yes, though sadly it looks as though she's not really had a good life despite her fame and money. Her real parents are dead. They were killed in a car crash when she was only eighteen months old. She was looked after by her mother's sister for a while, but then for some reason was adopted by a couple from Croydon.' Fabi paused, proffered a sad look and continued, 'It gets sadder. Angel's adopted mum died of breast cancer when she was fourteen. She never saw Angel become famous. Though her adopted dad did. He continued to bring her up though, again sadly, that wasn't for long either. They'd been in their forties when they'd adopted her, so by the time she'd become famous he was in his early sixties and was suffering from ill health.

He'd had one heart attack when she was seventeen, and then three years before her own death, he'd had another heart attack, which was fatal. Angel was just twenty when all that happened.'

'So she'd got no family?'

'It would appear not. Quite tragic don't you think?'

'Especially given that the one person she should have got comfort from turns out to be a bit of a twat. Excuse my French.'

Fabi smiled, 'You're excused.'

'And so following her death, Mathew Tobias Alexander gets his head down, does a disappearing act of his own, comes and lives our way, and changes his name to Toby.'

Fabi nodded thoughtfully, 'It would appear so.' Then with a big grin she said, 'Now I've shown you mine, you show me yours.'

17

'You're getting too cheeky young missy,' Jack responded with a smile, brushing aside Fabi's paperwork to reveal his handwritten notes underneath. Picking them up he said, 'Nothing earth-shattering to be honest. Not as much information as you've managed to get.' Scanning the pages quickly he shuffled one to the top. 'I've had difficulty tracking down Carrie. She certainly didn't fly into the UK via any of London's airports. I've had Immigration check twice, so I'm extending the checks and I'm incorporating European flights as well as Australian. And I'm also extending checks to see if she came overland from Europe..' He selected another note, 'Now, as to her financial details. She has a British bank account. It was set up in Penzance shortly after she moved to Cornwall with Mathew. She deposited eight-thousand-five-hundred-pounds in cash into the account, but has only drawn small amounts from it and those transactions have been irregular. So unless she has some other source of income, which I should know of soon, because I'm making an application to the courts, I'm working on the assumption that she has relied mostly on Mathew's money. From the account we know nothing has been drawn out of it for ten days. Her last withdrawal was just a hundred-pounds. Activity checks reveal this is usually the norm, so you would have thought that if she had done a runner to get away from Mathew she would have drawn more money out for food and somewhere to stay.'

'Unless she's got a bolt-hole somewhere or is staying with someone?'

'Or something's happened to her.' Jack swapped suspicious expressions with Fabi. There was a moments silence between them and then Jack said, 'Let's hold onto that thought, but there's still quite a bit of work to do before we up it to a murder enquiry. I've put a marker on her bank account to let me know the minute any money is drawn out and I've initiated an enquiry with Interpol to check if Carrie has returned to Australia. And we're awaiting her mobile location, or at least the last location it was used. Also there's her car. We still haven't traced that. ANPR hasn't picked it up on any of the road systems yet. Which, in itself, is a little unusual, don't you think?'

Fabi nodded, 'What about the media?'

'I've spoke to the DI and with the Press Department and we've agreed to hold off from releasing this for a few more days, especially given that we don't have any photographs of her. I've chased up the phone techies at Headquarters, who are up to their necks at the moment with computer stuff from a big drugs raid, but they've promised me that they should have something for us in another couple of days. If it throws up anything we don't like then we step things up a gear.'

18

Jack closed down his computer, picked his coat off the back of his chair, ran a final eye over his tidied desk, and left the CID office turning off the lights before closing the door. It was just after eight p.m. He was the last to leave the office which, given his normal working habit, wasn't unusual, though today he had deliberately delayed leaving for he knew sleep would be a long time coming – if at all.

As he made his way across the rear yard he reflected on his day. He felt guilty that his afternoon mawkishness, which still affected him, had impacted on Fabi. He had caught her staring at him shortly after 5p.m. She had instantly snatched away her gaze, but he hadn't missed her uncomfortable look. He had apologised for his behaviour, and although she had told him that it wasn't him, that she'd got an evening meal booked with Stephen, and was wondering what time they were clocking off, he had not been convinced of her response. He had apologised again, telling her that he had some personal paperwork to finalise before he called it a day, and that she should 'get herself off,' and with a fake smile, he had added, 'And make sure you have a good time, you never know in this job when the next opportunity will come,'

The comment about the paperwork had been a lie. He had nothing pressing. The bottom line was that he couldn't face his ghost house. So, in the quiet of the office, he had made himself a fresh cup and settled back, briefly re-visited the notes he and Fabi had made on Carrie, and then spent two hours with his head resting in his hands trying his best to shake away the images of his wife lying dead in the bath and thinking what turmoil she must have been going through to make her take her life the way she had. The thoughts of Clair had been triggered by Fabi revealing how Angel had died. The moment she had told him how Angel had been found surrounded by pills, his conscience was attacked and he'd had difficulty shifting the vision no matter how hard he had tried.

Back home Mollie greeted him the moment he stepped over the threshold, eagerly pushing against him to be fussed and more pangs of guilt overcame him. Not bothering to change he repaid his dog's greeting by taking to the streets with her for her evening walk. He covered most of the village inside twenty minutes and then took the track out towards Mousehole. The fields he tramped across were muddier than he had anticipated and he cursed every time he lifted a caked foot. At the same time, he knew that the walk was just what he needed to lift his spirits and so he picked up his pace. Ten minutes later, catching his breath, he looked back to gather his bearings. He could just make out the dim glow of one of Paul's edge-of-village streetlamps, making him realise he had come farther than intended, and with the way ahead offering only pitch darkness, he called Mollie to heel, patted her shoulder and headed back.

Three-quarters of an hour later, back in his hallway, he toe-heeled off his damp and muddy shoes, slipped off his jacket, slackened his tie then fed and watered Mollie. He made himself a cheese sandwich, poured himself a whisky and drifted into the lounge. He switched on the TV just in time to catch the late news. Within minutes he realised there was nothing of interest so he turned off the TV, tucked Mollie in her basket and made his way upstairs with his supper.

He ran a bath and went into his bedroom, dumping himself down on the edge of the bed, listening to water fill up the bath while he ate his sandwich and sipped his nightcap. Ten minutes later, putting down an empty plate and glass he undressed and returned to the bathroom for a long soak.

***

Jack couldn't sleep. No matter how hard he tried rest was elusive. For the umpteenth time he checked the illuminated clock on his bedside table, 3:12. Giving the clock another look with a heavy sigh, he decided it was pointless trying any more, and he flung aside the duvet, swung his legs out of bed and made his way to the back bedroom. Claire's room. Where she'd taken herself off to during her darkest periods. He switched on the light and waited for the temporary white blindness to fade. Within seconds, his sight readjusted, he began exploring her room – taking in the décor and sniffing the air. There was still the odd moment when he was certain he could still smell the floral bouquet of her perfume. Tonight, though, wasn't one of those times. He dropped his gaze. On the bed were photographs similar to the ones on the coffee table downstairs. Claire and himself, each one a memory that provoked a tug of his heartstrings. They began to blur as his eyes filled up. Picking up one of the photographs he clutched it to his chest, flopped onto his side and started to sob. *Why did you do this to me Claire? I miss you so much.*

19

Mathew Tobias Alexander checked his face in the bathroom mirror. He had two days of stubble and panda-like rings circled his bloodshot eyes. *I look as bad as I feel.* But that wasn't surprising, given his lack of sleep since his sighting of the mysterious stranger at the bottom of his garden and that phone call two nights ago.

Did someone know something, he wondered?

He had thought about it endlessly, more so since his interview with those two detectives. They were suspicious. He could tell. He had distinctly seen it in the man's eyes when he had questioned him as to whether he and Carrie had fought. The query had sent the hairs at the back of his neck on end and made him feel sick. Now, reminiscing on that had settled one thing in his mind – he had to completely get rid of any incriminating evidence. That day. Just in case.

He brushed his teeth, showered quickly and dressed in some of his old painting clothes. Then he made his way downstairs to the kitchen, filled up a bucket with boiling water, took out the bleach from under the sink, and, rolling up his sleeves he slipped on a pair of rubber gloves, lowered himself onto his knees and began hand washing the floor, pouring bleach as he scrubbed. He had seen it on CSI on TV. Bleach was the best way of getting rid of bloodstains. The next thing he needed to do was burn the clothes he'd been wearing last Sunday. Just in case.

20

At 6a.m. Jack had given up trying to get some sleep and got up and breakfasted, walked Mollie around the churchyard and then drove into work. The CID office was desolate, but on mornings like this when he needed to sort out his head he preferred it empty. Checking his watch, he knew that in half an hour this room would be full of chatter and he wanted to be prepared and in the mood for it. He slipped off his jacket, booted up his computer then walked to the far side of the office where the windows overlooked the rear car park, then he made a strong cup of tea before returning to his desk. Placing the steaming drink on a coaster he cracked back his fingers and opened up his e-mails. He was hoping there might be something there from the phone techies about Carrie's mobile location. There wasn't. With a sigh he closed them down and turned to his desk phone. Entering his code, he checked voicemail. There was one message waiting for him. He noted the time of the caller 8.45 last night. He had just missed it. He hit the play button and listened. The caller was female. The voice sounded young. Early twenties, he thought. She introduced herself as a friend of Angel's, though she didn't give her name. She spoke for thirty seconds. The intonation was brittle, nervous, disjointed, but the message she delivered gave him a burst of adrenalin and, on a high, he played it again, this time scribbling a few notes. The information she relayed sent his heartbeat racing. He was disappointed she hadn't left a number and he knew there was no way of getting one. He stored the call, pushed himself back in his chair and mulled on the significance of what he'd just heard.

He was still in that position quarter-of-an-hour later when Fabi arrived.

Dropping her bag and unbuttoning her overcoat she said, 'You look pleased with yourself.'

'This case has just taken a very interesting turn,' he replied slowly.

74

Draping her coat around her seat she pulled a mystified face, 'That's very cryptic Jack.'

Leaning forward he answered, 'Someone left me a very interesting message on my voicemail last night. Just listen to this.' Putting his phone on speaker he quickly punched in the dial-up number and code for his voicemail and waited for the message to play.

Within seconds the female voice, which had a London accent, began, 'I've been given this number, and been told you are looking into Mathew Alexander, about his girlfriend going missing. I don't know anything about that but I do know about what happened to Angel…' There was a pause. In the background Jack could make out lots of voices. They were indiscernible in terms of precise conversation, but they were part of significant background noise. It sounded as if the girl was in a pub. After a brief moment the she continued, '…Well I don't know exactly, but Pippa from the gallery does. You should speak to her. She knows what Mathew is like. It was what he did to her that caused them to argue that night Angel died. I don't think it's right what he did and got away with.' Then she hung up.

Listening to the burring sound of the ended message Fabi's eyebrows met. 'What Mathew did to who? Angel or Pippa?'

Jack shrugged and killed the call, 'I interpret it that the girl is telling us that Mathew did something to Pippa Johnson and that caused Angel and Mathew's bust-up on the night she died.'

'I wonder what that something was?'

'Well we'll soon find out. Fancy a trip to London again? I noticed when we were there that the gallery closes at 5.30p.m. We'll wait for Pippa to leave and see if we can talk to her without David Muir finding out. I don't trust him and I don't want this getting back to Mathew. Not just yet.'

***

Jack and Fabi got a late morning train from Penzance into London. They worked it out that they should be in Kensington a good hour before the gallery closed. They were hoping that, like many others who worked in the capital, Pippa wouldn't be using a vehicle but would make her way to the nearby underground station and travel home on the tube. They also hoped that she would leave first, and David, the owner, would be the one who locked up.

In the quiet carriage Jack and Fabi sat opposite each other, a table between them. Jack had his elbows resting on it, hands in a prayer-like gesture, staring out of the window at the countryside flying by.

Fabi eyed him closely. He appeared to be in deep thought and she thought that his gaze didn't seem to be going beyond his ghost-like reflection in the glass. She deliberately cleared her throat getting Jack's attention.

'Can I ask you something Jack?'

He gave her a quizzical look and dropped his hands onto the table.

'About your wife, Claire?'

She watched him studying her for a moment before responding with, 'What about Claire?'

'I don't mean to pry Jack, but what was behind what happened to her? How did she get depressed? If you don't mind me asking?'

For many seconds Jack's eyes never drifted from hers, then with a look of resignation he said, 'We lost a child. Our only child.'

'Oh I'm sorry Jack.'

He held up a hand, 'Don't be. It was one of those things. Just not meant to be. It was a long time ago.' For several seconds he was silent. His gaze drifted somewhere beyond Fabi's shoulder, then, locking eyes said, 'I was twenty-seven, Claire was a year younger. We'd been married five years and talked about having a family ever since getting together at eighteen. We tried for years and nothing seemed to happen so she went to the doctors. They referred her to the hospital and the specialist there found that Claire had a blocked fallopian tube. She had an operation and within a year got pregnant. We were over the moon.' For a moment his face lit up, then the corners of his mouth drooped. 'Six months into her pregnancy Claire felt something wasn't quite right. She couldn't feel the baby move and so went to the hospital. She was admitted and they discovered that the baby had died. Some genetic problem. Labour was induced but complications occurred and it damaged her womb. She couldn't have any more children.'

'Jack, that is so tragic.'

He momentarily stiffened, 'That was the start of her depression. I didn't realise at first because I was out long hours with the job. I'd got into CID. I just thought she was tired with what had happened to her, but then there were whole weeks when she wouldn't get out of bed. Wouldn't wash herself. I finally got her to see a doctor who prescribed her anti-depressants. But she just never got any better. She was referred to a psychiatrist and over the years she had to be admitted to the psyche ward on several occasions.'

'You must have had a terrible time. Both of you,' Fabi interjected.

Jack nodded, but it was half-hearted, 'To be honest I just wrapped myself up in my work. There were some days I couldn't face going home. Claire wasn't the person I married. Don't get me wrong she had some good days, but it was just that – days. Then, she'd be back to being depressed again. The last few years we didn't have a life, just an existence. Then, when she took her own life that day I felt so guilty, even though I knew deep down it wasn't my fault. If it hadn't been that day it would have been another. The counsellor I've been seeing told me that.'

So why should you feel guilty about it Jack?'

'I argued with Claire that day. I'd been working on a murder. Three weeks of fourteen hour days in a row and I was knackered. I tried to get her to get up before I went to work but she'd gone into one of her dark moods and I just snapped. I told her she needed to buck herself up. She was making my life a misery, and stormed out. I should have finished at five that day but couldn't face going home and so went to the pub.' He broke off for a few seconds, his gaze going distant. Then he brought it back to her, 'When I got home I found Claire like that. I just keep thinking if only I'd gone home, maybe I could have prevented it or saved her. I really regret what I did and I can't make amends.'

Fabi caught Jack's eyes starting to glass over and she reached across for his hands.

21

Fabi and Jack found a coffee shop on Kensington High Street, almost opposite the gallery and, although at an angle, the window seats they had secured gave them a decent enough view of the entrance to see and identify who came and went.

Jack checked his watch, noting that in less than an hour, according to the opening times on the sign, the gallery would close. He said to Fabi, 'I haven't seen any activity inside the place since we got here I hope Pippa's there. I don't want this to be a wasted journey.'

Fabi rested her lips on the wide brim of her cup. Looking over the top she replied, 'I'm sure she will be it's still open I saw a couple coming out of there as I sat down and you were ordering the coffees.'

Jack acknowledged with a nod and picked up his cup. For the best part of a minute he locked his eyes on the front door of the gallery, then he started to sweep his gaze. After a couple of minutes, he said, 'I'd hate to live here. It must be a nightmare. No peace and quiet, constant traffic congestion. Can you imagine what it must be like to police?'

'Oh I don't know about policing Jack. I bet it would be quite exciting.'

'If you were young, it would,' he interrupted.

She quickly lowered her cup, 'I am young, you cheeky devil.'

He let out a short laugh, then, his face changed. 'Hey up, eyes front, we've got movement.'

Fabi turned just in time to see Pippa Johnson closing the front door of the gallery. She stood, momentarily looking up and down the street, while fastening her coat around her. Finally, she hooked her bag onto her shoulder and headed their way.

Jack pulled himself back from the window and Fabi turned her back. Jack's view was over Fabi's shoulder and after thirty seconds he announced, 'She's gone past, come on, chop, chop.' He set down his half full cup and made for the door.

Fabi took a last quick slurp of her coffee and followed.

Outside, giving the gallery entrance door the final once over, satisfying himself that David wasn't following his assistant out of the premises, Jack immediately turned his attention on Pippa. Watching her stride ahead, it wasn't as he anticipated – she wasn't heading in the direction of the tube station, but in the opposite direction to Knightsbridge and she wasn't strolling. He set off after her at a smart clip, drawing his coat around him. Behind, he could hear the clop of Fabi's ballet pumps skipping across the pavement to catch him up. It didn't take her long. Within seconds she was by his side, the pair making progress as they outpaced Pippa's footwork. Within a couple of minutes, they had caught up opposite her. Jack checked the slow ribbon of traffic passing and with a shout of 'GO' made a dash, Fabi hanging on to his coat-tails. A couple of cars blasted their horns as they sprinted past their grills but it didn't impede their progress, and in less than five seconds they were leaping onto the footpath next to Pippa. She gave a startled jump and immediately went to grip her bag's shoulder strap. The look she engaged them with was one of recognition and she instantly released the hold on her bag.

'Sorry about that Pippa,' announced Fabi. 'We didn't mean to make you jump.'

'Jesus! You frightened the life out of me, I thought you were muggers.'

'Well we're not,' said Jack straight-faced.

From Pippa's expression Jack could see she had twigged that their being there wasn't for social pleasure.

'This is about Mathew isn't it?' She bounced her gaze from Jack to Fabi.

Both detectives nodded.

'We know what he did to you Pippa,' Jack half-lied. It was a wild card he was playing from the mysterious voicemail message he had listened to that morning.

She paled. 'Who told you?'

'We need to talk.'

22

Jack suggested a coffee shop a few streets away from the gallery - he wasn't sure he trusted David Muir and didn't want him seeing them. Pippa recommended one and showed them the way. The place she chose was relatively busy but they found a table toward the back and Jack went to order. Jack waited at the counter listening to the machine froth their coffees while Fabi sorted the table arrangements. She put herself in a position that forced Pippa to take a seat next to the wall; Pippa wasn't being detained, but Fabi wanted to make it awkward for her to leave until they had finished their chat

Jack watched her over his shoulder and smiled to himself. She was learning fast.

Pippa looked to be still in a state of shock as she unbuttoned her coat. 'It was Emma wasn't it?'

Fabi dropped down into her seat, 'Emma?'

Dragging out the chair next to her Pippa put down her bag and then laid her coat on top. Sitting down she replied, 'I don't know her second name. She was Angel's friend. They were from the same agency.'

Jack suddenly loomed above them, setting down three large Latte's and several sachets of sugar. Leaning in he said, 'We can't tell you who gave us the information Pippa. That would be unfair. You'll appreciate she chose to tell us anonymously.' He was still keeping up the pretence, although what he had just told her hadn't been untruthful. They didn't know who had left them the information on his voicemail, though they now had a starting point thanks to Pippa. He added, 'Look Pippa, you know we are in the middle of an enquiry to find Mathew's girlfriend who's mysteriously disappeared, and we now know that Mathew isn't being exactly honest with us. When we start these enquiries it generally throws up all kinds of information, which leads to uncomfortable questions for some. This information we have recently received leads us to you. Now we know Mathew did something to you and it would be really helpful if you were able to talk about it.' All the while he had been talking he had been locked on to Pippa's face, who was staring down at her coffee. She never once looked up to make eye contact. Jack noticed hive blotches beginning to appear around Pippa's neck – a clear sign she was nervous. In a soft tone he continued, 'We're not here to cause you embarrassment Pippa. All we want to do is get to the bottom of this. We believe Mathew is mixed up in something, not only to do with Carrie, but also his previous girlfriend Angel and we need all the help we can get.'

Pippa lifted her head. Her cheeks were red, 'I know it was Emma. She told you what Mathew did to me, didn't she? Only Emma knew. She was the one who told Angel, which caused the argument.'

Jack said, 'Look Pippa, As I've said, all we want to do is get to the bottom of this. We know people are hiding things and all that's doing is protecting Mathew, who we believe is up to his neck in things."

With tightened lips she replied, 'I told Emma not to tell anyone about this. I didn't want anyone else to know what Mathew was like. Not even Angel.' Her eyes were wide. 'It wasn't my fault. It was Mathew who attacked me.'

Fabi leaned across the table and covered her hands with her own, 'Pippa, we're here to support you.'

'I think Mathew raped me!' Pippa made a sharp intake of breath and pulled back her hands. 'There I've told you'

For a good few seconds the three watched each other's faces. Fabi was the first to break the silence.

'That's the hard part over Pippa. Now just tell us how it happened. In your own time.' More customers were coming into the shop, passing their table to get to the counter, and so Fabi lowered her voice.

For a good ten seconds Pippa flicked her eyes between Jack and Fabi. Then, taking a deep breath she responded, 'It was at a party six weeks before Angel died. It was at Emma's apartment. Mathew invited me. He came to the gallery with a couple of paintings and just said they were having a small get-together and it'd be good if I could come. To be honest I wasn't too sure about going because I didn't think I would know anyone, but Mathew said Angel would be there and he knew I used to chat with her when they came to the gallery so I agreed. I have to say it was amazing when I first got there. I recognised so many people from the cat-walk and there were a couple of actors there as well, it was great fun talking to them, but I'm not much of a drinker so I ended up just watching them getting off their faces and going into their own little cliques. About half-ten I'd decided I'd had enough and had just got my things to leave when Mathew stopped me in the hallway. He told me that Angel had crashed out drunk in one of the bedrooms and that he'd seen me drinking alone and thought I looked like I needed cheering up. We just started chatting.'

'What about?' asked Fabi.

'Mainly about art. He'd got an exhibition coming up. He was asking me what I thought about his latest work. Then he asked me if I wanted another drink. I told him I was thinking of going. He said something like "Oh don't go yet the party's just getting started." I said something about Angel, and he said, "She's out for the night now." He pressed me to have one last drink and I told him one more, then I'm going. I made an excuse that my parents would be expecting me home. He got me a gin and tonic and we chatted some more and that's when I started to feel funny.'

'Feel funny?' repeated Fabi.

'Yes, the room started spinning. It was really weird, like I was having this out of body experience. It just happened so quick. I could feel my heart racing. It was awful. And then that was it. The next thing I remember was coming round, lying on this bed and Mathew was looking down at me. He was pulling on his trousers. My dress was half undone and I didn't have any knickers on. I just knew what he'd done to me.'

Fabi took on a look of concern. For a few seconds she said nothing. Then she asked, 'Did you say anything to Mathew, or do anything?'

'I wasn't in a fit state and my head was all over the place. I knew what was happening but couldn't function properly. It was horrible. I asked him what he'd done to my drink and he just started laughing. I said 'You've raped me haven't you.''

'What was his reaction to that?'

He just looked at me and said, 'I'd been begging for him all night. That's what he would tell everyone if I said anything.'

'So what did you do?'

'I got mad. Said I was going to tell Angel what he'd done. That's when he grabbed me.'

'Grabbed you?'

'Yes, got hold of me by the arms. Started shaking me. He was really angry. He scared me. I'd never seen him like that. He told me that no one would believe me and that he would make sure I lost my job and that my father would find out. My Dad's an executive with an American Bank and knows a lot if influential people. I didn't want to cause him any embarrassment. Mathew knew that.'

'Did you ask him about the drink he'd given you?'

She nodded, 'I said to him "you put something in my drink, didn't you?" He just laughed at me again and told me to prove it.'

On a caring note Fabi said, 'And is that when you told Emma?'

Pippa shook her head, 'No, I didn't tell anyone about what happened. Not for ages. If I knew Mathew was coming to the gallery, I'd make an excuse and not be there when he came in.'

'So when did you tell Emma?'

'It was a few days before Angel died. I was in a bar with friends one Friday evening and Emma came in with a couple of her friends. Angel wasn't with her. She started talking to me, and told me that Angel was getting engaged to Mathew, and wasn't that great? I just said that she wouldn't if she knew what he was like. I couldn't stop myself. Once it came out that was it, I just told Emma what he'd done to me that night at the party.'

'What did Emma say?'

'What do you think? She was gob-smacked! She asked me if I'd told anyone? If I'd told Angel? I said she was the only person I'd told. She just said, "I'd keep this to yourself if I was you" and then left with her friends. But the next day I had Angel on the phone at the gallery screaming and shouting at me. Calling me a slapper. Emma had told her. It was awful. I was glad David wasn't in when she rang.'

'Gosh Pippa, what did you say to her? Did you tell her what had happened?'

Pippa nodded her head vigorously, 'Yes. I had to defend myself. I wasn't the one to blame. It was Mathew. I told her what he'd done that night at the party. That he'd put something in my drink and raped me.'

'Did Angel say anything else to you?'

'Only that I was to stay away from her. Never talk to her again. Then she hung up. She made me feel terrible, as though it was my fault.'

'And did you ever see Emma again and speak with her.'

'Not until after Angel died.' She took a deep sigh. 'David told me the morning they found her. I couldn't believe it. I thought deep down it might have something to do with what happened to me.'

'But you still never told anyone what Mathew had done? Even when you knew the police were investigating Angel's death?'

'I was scared. Terrified in fact.'

'And did you speak with Emma?'

Pippa nodded. 'I saw her a couple of weeks before the inquest. She was waiting for me one evening when I'd left work. She said she wanted a word with me. She asked me if I'd told anyone about what had happened. I told her only her and she said she felt terrible about what had happened to Angel. She said she'd told Angel what Mathew had done to me because she felt so bad about things. She apologised to me because she knew Angel had slagged me off and she knew it wasn't my fault. She said that if it was anyone's fault, it was Mathew's. I asked her what Angel had said when she'd told her about me? She said that at first Angel had refused to believe it, but then a couple of days later Angel told her she was going to have it out with him and call off the engagement. That she'd never be able to trust him again. She was going to tell him the night before she was found dead. I think that was what their argument was about.'

'But you never told the police about this?'

'The police only spoke with David.'

'And so you didn't give evidence at the inquest?'

Pippa shook her head. 'They never called me. I looked after the gallery while David went. He gave me feedback.'

'You know your information could have been vital don't you? It would have given the coroner a reason why she took her own life when he delivered his verdict.'

'It wouldn't have made any difference though would it? It would still have been a suicide verdict.'

'And do you think it was suicide?'

Pippa shrugged. 'I think so. I have to say, there have been some moments when I've thought about what Mathew did to me, and I've wondered if he'd got nasty with Angel, and that caused her to overdose and that's how she died.'

23

Outside the coffee shop Jack and Fabi said their goodbyes to Pippa and watched her slowly stroll away. In a matter of seconds she had gone – swallowed up by the throng of commuters all making their way to bars or home. Evening was taking hold over London. A warm yellow glow dominated the skyline signifying the onset of dusk.

Jack pulled on his overcoat, 'Do you think we did the right thing there?'

'You mean letting her go without taking a statement from her?'

Jack nodded, 'She was very brave in there Fabi. She's kept that bottled up for so long. Somehow she blames herself for what happened. I could see it in her eyes while she was answering your questions. The last thing she wants now is us pressuring her to give a statement. It could tip her over the edge. I don't want another suicide on my hands. We know where to find her. If we need her evidence, we'll do a softly-softly approach in a couple of weeks. Sit down with her and explain how much we need her help.' Jack checked Fabi's look. 'What do you think?'

Fabi offered a tight lipped smile, 'I think you're right. But I'd love to drag Mathew's arse down to the station. It's shocking what he's done to her. He can't get away with that.'

'He won't, don't worry. He'll get what's coming to him. Believe me. But now, we need to speak with this Emma girl. We've got her address from Pippa. I'm going to get hold of the gaffer, tell him what we've got and that we need a stay over to finalise our enquiries. We'll catch the train back tomorrow.' Jack threw her a questioning look, 'Unless you have something pressing back home with that partner of yours?'

Fabi issued a soft smile. 'No I'll give Stephen a call. He knows this is important to me – how much I've wanted CID. We'll catch up this weekend.'

'Good that's the type of partner you need.' Jack rubbed his hands together, 'Now what about something to eat. We'll check on Emma's details and address and then we'll nip over and have a little chat with her.'

Jack set off without warning, catching Fabi unawares, and she found herself doing a double-shuffle before jogging after him, cursing, as she almost tripped over her own feet.

***

Emma Kirby was listed in the voters' register. She lived in a luxury apartment in Southwark, overlooking the Thames. As Jack entered the huge marble and glass reception area he couldn't but help be impressed. This was serious money he thought, as he approached a smartly dressed female sitting behind reception. Flashing his warrant card, he told the young woman who they were and said they were here to talk with Miss Kirby. Holding up a finger, she indicated for them to wait one moment and then made a phone call. After a few seconds, Jack listened to the receptionist telling whoever was on the other end of the line that two detectives were here and wished to speak with her. A couple of seconds later she removed the phone from her ear, covered the mouthpiece and said, 'Miss Kirby is enquiring what it's about?'

Jack answered, 'Will you tell her it's in connection with a missing woman.'

The receptionist went back on the phone, delivered his message and then hung up. Lifting herself out of her chair she said, 'Miss Kirby said she doesn't know how she can help you but she's willing to speak with you.' Leaning across the counter she pointed the way down toward a lift area and said, 'Miss Kirby lives on the eleventh floor, apartment 75.'

Jack thanked her and made his way past the front of reception, Fabi tucked herself bedside him.

As they rode the lift Jack nudged Fabi. 'This is a bit different to the flats I'm used to visiting, 'scuse my French, but the lifts I go in usually smell of stale piss or cannabis.'

Fabi let out a laugh as the elevator slowly came to a halt at the 11th floor. As the doors pinged open, she stepped out into the corridor. She said, 'You need to get out more Jack.'

Apartment 75 was through a set of double doors and just around the first corner. Emma Kirby opened the highly polished oak door to Jack's first knock.

Jack found himself greeting a tall, slender black woman, with glossy, ebony shoulder length hair and healthy-looking skin. She was wearing black skinny jeans, which accentuated the length of her legs, and a red silk vest. He immediately found himself captivated by her beauty and glamour but, masking his admiration, he held up his identification and introduced himself and Fabi. He said, 'We'd like to ask you a few questions about Mathew Alexander, or you might know him as Toby Alexander.'

Emma Kirby gave them a sour glance. 'The receptionist downstairs said it was about a missing woman.'

As she finished her sentence Jack recognised that it had been her voice on his voicemail. Watching her face carefully he answered, 'It is, sort of. But it's also got something to do with Mr Alexander. We've just spent the last couple of hours with Pippa, from the gallery and she's told us a very interesting story.' He paused for a split second and then added, 'But then you know that because you left me a message on my voicemail yesterday pointing me in her direction.' Jack thought he caught her face flushing.

She cleared her throat and said, 'You'd better come in.'

Jack had been impressed with the plush reception area, but the interior he was now casting his eyes over completely blew him away. He was amazed by how huge and bright the apartment was. Large windows ran the entire length of one wall and extended into the right hand corner of the room giving a panoramic view of the cityscape overlooking the Thames. He recognised the iconic Shard building, St.Paul's Cathedral and Tower Bridge.

Emma indicated a large cream leather sofa to them and sat herself down on an identical one opposite. Sitting back and hooking one arm over the low cushions she said, 'How is Pippa?'

Fabi answered, 'Pippa's fine. Surprisingly.'

'She told you everything?'

'That Mathew had raped her?'

Emma acknowledged Fabi's response with a nod. 'It wasn't right. I should have told someone about what Mathew had done a long time ago. I should have mentioned what he was like at the inquest but I was warned off.'

'Warned off?' Interjected Jack.

Emma pursed her mouth. 'Well, not exactly warned. That's a bit strong. But Samuel and Deanna who run the agency said they couldn't afford bad publicity. They didn't know about the incident involving Pippa, but obviously what had happened to Angel had been terrible, and they said they didn't want any scandal, and so they suggested that me and the others that were called to give evidence should just tell the police what type of person Angel was and leave it at that.' Pausing and switching her gaze between them she continued, 'You know – about her personality and that kind of thing. I told Deanna what I knew about Angel and Mathew arguing but she said unless I'd actually witnessed it, that I shouldn't invite trouble. Deanna and Samuel were especially uncomfortable with Angel's drug use and what impact that could have. They said unless I was specifically asked about that, to just say I hadn't seen her use drugs. Which wasn't a lie exactly. So I told that detective who was investigating her death just what Angel was like as a person and left it at that.'

'But it wasn't only Emma, was it? You knew about what had happened to Pippa. You knew what Mathew had done to her, because she told you. And you told Angel. And you also knew that Angel was going to have it out with Mathew on the night before she died, because she told you she was going to. Why didn't you tell the detective that?'

Suddenly she looked uncomfortable. She stuttered over her words at first, then she replied, 'I didn't know for definite Angel had rowed with Mathew. She told me she was going to challenge him about it, but I wasn't there so I didn't know if she did or not.'

Raising his voice Jack responded, 'Emma that's rubbish. The inquest was told that Angel and Mathew had argued on the night she died, because a neighbour heard them. You had an opportunity to tell the coroner what you believed to be behind their argument.'

Emma shied her eyes away. She was silent for a brief time and then replied, 'I know. You're right. I should have, but I didn't. Some of it was me being scared and some it was about protecting me and the agency. That's why I left that message for you.'

'Emma, why did you ring us now after all this time?' It was Fabi who asked.

'I've been feeling so guilty. I know deep down I should have said something, so when I heard about Mathew's girlfriend being missing, I thought this was my time to make amends.'

'How did you find out about this? There's been no publicity.'

'I bumped into David Muir a couple of days ago and he told me that Mathew was under investigation again. I don't know, but something just set the alarm bells ringing. With what happened to Angel and now this with his new girlfriend. And then of course what he did to Pippa.'

Fabi said, 'You think that he's done something to his girlfriend then?'

She shrugged her shoulders. 'I'm not sure. I don't know the circumstances of her disappearance. David didn't tell me. He just said she'd gone missing and that you're investigating it.'

'But am I right in thinking that you believe Mathew might have something to do with her disappearance.'

'Only because of how he was with Angel.'

Jack leaned forward and took up the questioning. 'What do you mean by that Emma?'

She removed her arm from the back of the sofa, pulled herself forward and dropped it down onto her lap, clasping her hands together she answered, 'Well I never witnessed anything, but I did see some bruising once to her neck and arms. She'd tried to cover it up with foundation but you could see what it was and she blushed and put on a sweat top when she saw me looking. This is why I feel so guilty. I know I have should have said something.'

'Tell us more.'

'You know all about Mathew and his paintings of Angel. But have you been told how they came to be together and what he was like with her?'

Jack raised his eyebrows. 'No one's told us anything. David Muir was the first person to tell us about Mathew and Angel when we went to his gallery three days ago. He didn't say much about their relationship other than what had happened to Angel. And to be fair, we didn't go much into it. But we've since found out quite a bit from our enquiries. We'd appreciate it if you'd tell us what you know?'

She sucked in a deep breath. Exhaling slowly, she said, 'As I say, you know about Mathew and his painting. There's no doubt he was good at what he did and you've seen what Angel was like, haven't you? She was beautiful.'

Jack and Fabi acknowledged with a nod.

'She met Mathew just as she was starting to get her face known. We joined the agency at about the same time and so we did quite a lot of things together. That's how we became friends. At the London fashion week in two-thousand-and-nine one of the main designers took a shine to Angel, and that was it. Within weeks she was in all the magazines and a make-up firm also came in and picked her up. She did some adverts for eye-liner and lip gloss. You might have seen them?'

Fabi had. She nodded.

'Well that's where Mathew came on to the scene. He knew someone from the commercial side of the make-up company and he was at the launch party of the eye-liner she was promoting. They got chatting, he told her he was an artist who painted portraits and he asked her if she'd come to his studio and let him paint her. It was as simple as that. She never thought it was going to be like it was. She told me she was only going because she was fascinated to see how an artist would paint her. There wasn't any relationship between them at first. He just painted her. Then, about six months after they met she told me that Mathew was having an exhibition of her portraits and she asked me if I'd go with her to the opening. Free champers, she said, so I couldn't resist. When I got there I could see there was more than a friendship between them and she just came out with the fact that they were seeing each other. I was pleased for her because Angel struggled with guys. With Mathew she seemed really happy.' She paused, looked at both detective's and said, 'Well she was at first, but pretty soon the old Angel was back and sometimes twice as bad.'

'What do you mean by that?' asked Jack.

'Well you know what she could be like, don't you? Some of it came out in the inquest.'

'We never went to the inquest Emma. We only know snippets of it.'

'Well, Angel could be difficult at times. Sometimes she was high as a kite and the next thing low as anything.'

'On drugs?'

Emma shook her head. 'Not at first. I've heard it was some kind of personality disorder. We used to talk about it when Angel wasn't around. Us girls. One of the girls said she had a cousin who'd got bipolar disorder, and she acted exactly like Angel did. To be honest, when I first got to know her it was something you just accepted about her and you'd stay clear of her when she went off on one. As I became friends with her I used to make a joke the moment she flipped and she'd calm down. I know others found her difficult.'

'Emma, you've just said you thought her moods weren't due to drugs, but then contradicted yourself. At the inquest the police presented evidence of her drug use. She had class A in her system and they found evidence of cocaine at her apartment.'

'Oh yes, it's no big secret, she did take drugs. What I mean is that at first it wasn't drugs. It genuinely was her personality. The drug use came when she was with Mathew. I found that out by accident. She wouldn't dare tell me because she knew I was dead against them. You see I lost a friend when I was eighteen. She took ecstasy at a club one night and collapsed. Went into a coma.' She engaged eyes with Fabi. 'It was awful! I was there when her parents had to make the decision to turn off her life support. That moment stayed with me, and ever since I've been a bit of a crusader against drugs, so when she confided in me once that she'd taken coke at a party with Mathew I flipped. She wouldn't tell me anything more after that, but some of the girls said they'd seen her use the stuff at parties they'd been to, and there were a couple of times when she turned up for a shoot worse for wear and Deanna had to send her home. I think she was given a warning once.' She let out a sigh. 'To be honest when I went to the inquest and heard that evidence – the fact that she had coke in her system – it wasn't a surprise, but the fact that she was on anti-depressants was. I knew she was having a rough time with Mathew towards the end but I didn't know it was that bad.' She shook her head. 'You see things weren't the same between us. She'd stopped telling me things because she knew what I was like about the drugs thing.'

Fabi said, 'Just digressing from that Emma, what about when Pippa confided in you about what Mathew had done to her?'

'At first, when she told me, I was shocked and angry. Not just about what he'd done to Pippa but for Angel as well. I knew things weren't right with her. I could see she was depressed. Pippa telling me what Mathew had done to her made me wonder if he was giving Angel a bad time as well and that's why she was like she was. I just thought, what a bastard, and I thought Angel should dump him. Especially as I also knew she was thinking about getting engaged to him. Others at the agency were talking about how she was going on about getting a ring and I just thought she should be confronted with the truth about what kind of person she was getting hitched to.'

'So how did she react when you told her?'

'She went mental at first. Said I was lying. That Pippa was lying. That Mathew wasn't like that. That Pippa must have led him on. That's when she phoned Pippa up and gave her a slagging. I felt awful about it. I felt bad for Pippa. I mean Mathew had done that to her and she was getting the blame for it from Angel.'

For several seconds there was silence between the three of them. Then Jack said, 'Emma you mentioned earlier the bruising you'd seen. Did you ever ask her how that happened?'

She nodded. 'I didn't at the time but I did a couple of weeks later. We were on a shoot together. I just asked her straight out how she'd come by them. She acted all dumb at first asking me what I was talking about, and I just said "come off it Angel anyone can see they're grip marks on your arms and neck". At first she didn't want to say anything and so I just said "Mathew's done that, hasn't he?" She was embarrassed about it, but she told me he had. She said they'd had this big bust up. That she'd said something about him using coke, like he was and he'd gone off on one at her. She told me that she was thinking of leaving him. To be honest I wasn't that sympathetic with her. I've already told you what I'm like about drugs. I just told her he wasn't worth it and to dump him – she could do better. She said she'd like to but she was afraid of him.'

'Afraid of him? She used those words?'

Emma nodded, 'Definitely. I said, just tell Samuel and Deanna and they'll get someone in to protect you. She said she knew that, but I didn't know what he could be like. That he had a nasty streak. She told me that she'd seen him once give a guy a good hiding just for coming up and talking to her and asking her for her autograph while they were out together. She'd had to drag him off and then they had this blazing row during which she'd threatened to leave him. Apparently he'd said to her "if you do I'll kill you."'

'When did he say this?'

Emma's eyes momentarily drifted up to the ceiling. Returning then a couple of seconds later she said, 'It would've been about three weeks before I found out what he'd done to Pippa, so that'd be about month before Angel was found dead.'

24

In an electrically charged CID office DI Dick Harrison took up the only empty seat at the head of the oval conference table. The seven other chairs were taken up by detectives from his squad. He had called them all together for a noon briefing following the phone call from Jack the previous evening. Shuffling forward, he tapped a bundle of papers he was holding into alignment and set down each sheet as if he was playing black-jack. Clearing his throat, he said, 'Okay scrum-down everyone, let's see what we've got.' He cast his eyes around, checking he had everyone's attention and continued, 'Carrie Jefferies; early thirties, believed to originate from Australia, and currently living at Merthen Point; disappeared nine days ago, on Sunday the twenty-sixth of April, but she was only reported missing four days ago by a friend.' He paused, looked at Jack and added. 'I believe I've got that right, and I'm now going to hand things over so you can fill us in as to the circumstances of her disappearance and to tell us what you've got to date.'

Jack steepled his fingers, resting the tips against his chin, and began summarising the status of his and Fabi's enquiry by outlining the first conversation they'd had with Tammy Callaghan at the police station when she reported Carrie missing. He briefed his colleagues as to the argument at the Callaghan's and how, since the early hours of Sunday morning, Carrie had not been heard of, and that no one, including him, had been able to contact her. He reported that there was no longer a signal from her mobile. Pausing, then moving on, he mentioned his and Fabi's visit to the cottage where she was living with Mathew Tobias Alexander, and how, during this meeting, Mathew had confirmed that he and Carrie had argued. How he had awoken the next day to find that Carrie had taken her car and handbag and he had not seen or heard from her since. Jack went on to outline the information he had gleaned from David Muir regarding the incident involving Angel May, imparting what his partner, Fabi, had uncovered following her enquiries, specifically detailing the nature of Angel's death and the subsequent inquest verdict. He said, 'Following the inquest Mathew changed his name to Toby and moved to his present address.' He continued, telling them of his mysterious voicemail, which had led them to speak with Pippa. 'She told us that she believed the phone call had been made by a woman called Emma Kirby, who was a friend of Angel's. Fabi and I managed to track her down last night and Pippa was spot-on. It was Emma who left me that message.' After enlightening everyone as to what these two had told them he leaned back in his seat releasing a satisfied smirk.

The DI took back the briefing. 'Thank you for that Jack,' and, eyeing Fabi, added 'Well done you two. I think you'll all agree we have something which warrants following up.' Glancing at his documents he pulled aside the top sheet, 'Okay, intelligence. You've told us about the circumstances of her disappearance, but what do we know about Carrie? I'm looking to you again Jack?'

'We've hit the buffers on this one. The possessions which would help us with that, her passport, driving licence and her personal laptop, according to Mathew, were all taken by her. Fabi and I have done an initial search of the house but there are no signs of any of them. The only thing she left behind is her clothing. So what we're left with is just what Mathew and the Callaghan's have told us about her. And from that we think Carrie is thirty-three years old and she originates from Australia. We don't know if she has any middle names. We don't know what family she has, and we don't have an address for her other than we are told she lives in New South Wales.' He looked around the table, 'For the uninitiated New South Wales is over three times the size of the UK so we've had our work cut out trying to trace her. In fact, we've been unsuccessful on that count with the authorities' down-under.'

'What about social media?' Detective Sergeant Gail Simpson asked, lifting her pen from her note pad and looking up.

Jack had been watching her doodling all through his briefing, though it hadn't concerned him, because he knew from experience that it was a habit of hers and that in reality she was taking everything in while she was sketching away. He answered, 'I'm not saying she's not registered on any of the sites but we haven't found her with the information we've got. There are a number of Carrie Jefferies listed, but none with her background. The other problem we have, which has complicated matters, is that we don't really know what she looks like. We have a verbal description from Mathew and the Callaghan's but we've not been able to find a photo of her anywhere. True, we have the paintings that Mathew's done of her, but because of his style, they don't help. No one we've talked to so far has ever taken a photo of her.'

'Isn't that strange don't you think?' It was Gail Simpson again. She had a knotted expression.

Jack nodded. 'I have to agree with you there, Serge. And, there are other things we've discovered that we found a little strange about this case.' Jack paused briefly and then said, 'We've done the normal phone requests, based on the number we've got for her and the info we've got back from the techies is not what we expected. The thing that especially stands out is the limited number of people she's called. I can count them on one hand. The only people she's telephoned from her mobile are her boyfriend, Mathew Alexander, Tammy Callaghan and David Muir. That's it. And you'd have thought, especially given that she's from Australia, that she'd have least phoned someone there. But no.' he shrugged his shoulders. 'That's not the only thing. Now there might be a completely innocent explanation for this, but the only bank account we've found in her name is the one here in the UK. In fact, it's one she set up here in Penzance shortly after she moved in with Mathew twelve months ago, and that was set up with a cash sum of eight-and-a-half-thousand pounds. No foreign or on-line transactions. And, I know it's still early doors with our enquiries but I thought we'd have found more about Carrie Jefferies than this.'

'So what is it you're suggesting Jack?' interjected DI Dick Harrison.

Looking nonplussed he replied, 'Well, as I say, I know it's early doors, but given the total lack of information we have about her, and the difficulties we're having tracing her back in Australia, it's almost as if before she came on the scene at Mathew Alexander's exhibition, she didn't exist.'

The DI threw Jack a questioning look. It lasted a brief moment before changing. Rubbing his hands, he said, 'Okay we'll hold that thought. It's something, that as a team, we can work on over the next few days. For now, there're more pressing things to do. First things first. Have we managed to get a trace on Carrie's phone?'

Jack gave a quick nod, 'Her phone stopped pinging six days ago so we think that the batteries are dead, but the last triangulation point they've managed to trace it to is on the old Boskenna estate.'

'That's only a few miles from Mathew Alexander's place isn't it?'

Jack responded to the Di's question with a sharp flick of his head.

'So that means that in the three days before her phone went down, she, or her phone, had not gone very far at all.'

Jack agreed with another nod.

'Okay, then the priority is to get that area searched. It's a big place so I'll need to bring in extra resources.' Roaming his eyes around the table, engaging a thoughtful look, he said, 'Right ladies and gents, as from now, I'm declaring this a major incident. On the one hand Carrie Jefferies could simply just have had enough and left, but given that, as far as we know, there is no other person in Carrie's life, except Mathew Alexander, and given what Jack has told us about what happened to Mathew's other girlfriend, Angel, what he did to Pippa Johnson, the nasty streak in his character, which Emma and the Callaghan's have both mentioned, I'm more inclined to think she's a victim. Either abducted or murdered, and therefore I'm going to step things up. Tomorrow morning, we begin a search of the Boskenna estate, and we bring in Mathew Alexander for questioning and carry out a forensic search of his house.'

25

Mathew Tobias Alexander sat in The Lamorna Wink pub staring at the last dregs of his second beer. He had gone to the old smugglers inn to seek solace and distraction from his nightmares of recent days but so far had found neither. When he had initially entered he had been surprised to see so many customers in the place, and he'd had to drink his first pint at the bar. It had been twenty minutes before a table became available and, as he watched the family departing from it, he quickly ordered another beer while grabbing the vacant slot. Then, pushing aside the dirty plates to make room for his pint, he hunkered over his glass and people-watched, trying his best to listen in on some of their conversation. But that hadn't lasted long. His concentration fragmented as thoughts of Carrie invaded his focus, and then somehow that had been replaced with images of his interrogation by those two detectives. At least it had felt like interrogation, though he knew it hadn't been. Suddenly, a fit of shaking overwhelmed him, dragging him back to the moment, re-fixing his thoughts and returning to his beer he finished off his pint in one swallow. As he set down his empty glass he knew he needed another, if only to chase away his haunting thoughts, and so he returned to the bar. As he eyed the pumps advertising the different hand-pulled ales his eyes drifted to the back of the bar where the optics were hung and he decided he could actually do with a whisky. A double. He ordered it with ice and a dash of lemonade and returned to his seat where he swirled the ice around the honey coloured contents and savoured the essence of the spirit as he returned to people-watching and listening. Ten minutes later it was gone, giving him an all-overwarm feeling and he ordered another, telling himself this would be his last. Although he wasn't far from home, at this time of the year the police didn't usually patrol his route, and the one thing he didn't want to happen, with everything that was going on right now, was to be pulled up and breathalysed, and so he took a little longer with this drink, eating a bag of crisps and a packet of peanuts in between. Seeing that it was coming up to nine p.m he set his empty tumbler down on the bar, slipped on his coat and made to leave the pub. But, before he stepped outside he had a change of mind and took a detour to the gents, which he checked was empty and he locked himself in a cubicle. Although the beer and whisky had taken the edge of his morose mood he still needed a hit so, reaching inside his coat he took out a small paper sachet, set it on top of the cistern, delicately unfolded it revealing the compacted white powder and arranged it into a thin strip. Taking a glass tube from the same pocket and inserting it up one nostril he pressed shut the other with his finger and took a sharp sniff of the cocaine. Lifting back his head he took another sniff, wiped the bottom of his nose, flushed the small envelope down the toilet and left the cubicle making his way to the exit. Outside, a fine drizzle was falling creating a thin mist and everything was in eerie relief. The glow from the few street lights that there were on the narrow hamlet road, was partially blocked by the fresh spring canopy of the trees lining either side, adding to the ghostly atmosphere. Shuddering, he unlocked his car, gathered his coat around him and climbed into the driver's seat, starting the engine before he'd made himself comfortable. The windscreen was misted over, so he revved the accelerator, cranked up the demister and let off a deep sigh as he settled. The rush from the cocaine was beginning. He could feel his heart picking up a pace and hear the blood hissing behind his ears. He adjusted the interior mirror to take a glimpse of himself. The reflection staring back was not a pretty one. He had several day's growth and dark rings around his eyes; his disturbed sleep pattern of the last few days was beginning to show. Sharply re-setting the mirror and seeing that the windscreen had cleared he belted up and set off with a wheel-spin, churning up the loose gravel at the front of the pub.

Within minutes he was out of Lamorna, heading up the dark winding lane which skirted the old Boskenna estate, keeping a keen eye open for oncoming headlights, although the roads were generally traffic free at this time he didn't want to take any chances and he hugged the nearside of the road. At the top of the incline he slowed for the junction, saw that there were no oncoming lights and, without stopping, made a hard left in the direction of his cottage.

On the top road he picked up speed and very quickly the landscape either side became a dark blur. The only things he could pick out were those directly in front, where the beam played on the narrow road, and so he eased off slightly and glanced in his rear view mirror. For a brief moment he thought he caught movement and he eased off even more, giving the road behind another glimpse but, seeing nothing, he geared down and squeezed on the accelerator again. However, the episode had spooked him and so he took to looking more in his mirrors – swapping nervously between interior and exterior. Another half a mile along and he caught the movement again. A pair of sidelights a few hundred yards behind. His heart began to palpitate and the hairs on his neck began to bristle. *The cops! I've had far too much to drink. And the coke.* Gripping the steering wheel tighter, he began edging up his speed. He was only five minutes from home and he knew these roads like the back of his hand. If it was the police he needed to put some distance between them, and with two litres of turbo engine under his bonnet that shouldn't be a problem he told himself. Wrapping his fingers tighter round the wheel he began throwing his ever speeding car into the tight bends. Despite the terror welling up inside he felt pumped up and he could feel the racing of his engine matching the cadence of his heart. Ahead he knew there was a series of bends, within them was his own turning to freedom and he willed the car faster. As he threw the car into the next bend, without warning, a bright beam of light hit his interior mirror, dazzling him and making him jump. For a split-second he could see nothing but fire-flies dancing behind his eyes and he went into a panic. He stamped on the brake, and in that instant the car started to slide. He blinked, returning his sight, and he immediately saw that he was on collision course with the wall on the opposite side of the road. He yanked down on the steering wheel to bring the car back under control. It didn't work. The car started to crab, the offside wheels hitting the verge, jarring the chassis and bouncing it sideways. Terrifyingly, he could see the roadside wall looming. Letting out a desperate cry he made one final pull on the steering to avoid the crash, but there was no traction and he smashed into the flint and granite blocks with a massive explosion of force. Glass detonated everywhere and bursting airbags stung his hearing, creating meteoric flares inside his head. Feeling himself lapsing into unconsciousness he tried forcing open his eyes. He thought he saw a car's headlight's pulling up beside him and a dark shape emerging. For the briefest of moments, he thought that the silhouette standing outside looked like the person he'd seen at the bottom of his garden and then everything went black.

26

The ringing of the bedside phone jerked Jack Buchan awake. Zipping open his eyes, he was surprised how dark it was and for a split-second anxiousness overcame him. Then quickly scrambling together his thoughts and trying to adjust his sight he snatched up the handset and answered with a gruff, 'Hello.'

'Good morning Jack.' It was DI Harrison. There was a note of sarcasm in his voice.

'Morning. Is it morning? It's still dark.'

It's half past six – it's morning.'

Jack let out a tired groan 'I'm guessing something's happened?'

'You bet. We've found Carrie's mini. It's been burnt out.'

Still trying to regulate his vision in the dark Jack propped himself up on one elbow. 'Where?'

'In the Boskenna Estate. In the woods. I rang the night-shift Inspector last night and asked his team to keep an eye out for it during their patrols. A couple on his team found it this morning. It's been found a fair way into the woods and it's been fired. The scenes been secured and I'm on my way down there now. I want you to join me.' There was a slight pause and then he said, 'And guess what? Mathew Alexander's in hospital. He crashed his car last night. Traffic are dealing. Haven't got the full sp yet but it looks like he was drunk.' After another pause he added, 'And give Fabi a ring will you. She might as well join us. This is her job as well.'

The DI ended the call and for a few seconds Jack listened to the soft burr, re-running in his head what the DI had just imparted. Then, switching on the bedside light he returned the phone to its holder and, spurring into action, threw aside the duvet and swung his legs out of bed.

***

Inside twenty minutes Jack was locking the front door and getting into his car. He had called Fabi while watching Mollie doing her toilet circuit of the rear garden, passing on to her the information the DI had given him and telling her to meet him at the crime scene.

Leaving Paul and entering the countryside Jack's attention was momentarily diverted by the sight of the awakening sun appearing above the hedgerows. It had been a long time since he had set off to work at this time and because of his recent illness he'd forgotten how beautiful and refreshing the dawn looked. In that moment he felt his mood lifting and he switched his thoughts to the job he was travelling to.

At the lay-by, close to The Merry Maidens ancient stone circle, he pulled in and made a call on his BlackBerry. Although he was familiar with the huge Boskenna Estate, much of it was enveloped by woodland with many entrances, and he needed to know exactly where everyone was.

DI Harrison answered within a couple of rings and gave him directions to a farm track that led to the 17th Century Mansion house in the middle of the estate. 'We're about a hundred yards down that track and off to your right. The entrance has been sealed off and one of the uniform's there is doing the log. See you shortly.' With that he hung up.

Dropping the phone onto the passenger seat, Jack set off in search of his destination. He soon found it, a line of parked police vehicles marked the location. The CSI van was the first vehicle he spotted, rear-guarding half a dozen others and, slowing down, he pulled in behind and parked up. Climbing out, he looked among the cars and saw that Fabi hadn't yet arrived, he checked his watch and, noting the time, he made the decision not to wait for her. Opening his boot, he slipped off his overcoat, climbed into his white protective suit, swapped his shoes for hiking boots and feet coveralls, then he locked the car and set off to where blue and white police tape signified the entrance to the crime scene.

The tape was fastened between two trees on opposite sides of a dirt road, forming a loose barrier and protecting the setting. A male constable in high-visibility clothing was lolling against one of the trees looking bored. On seeing Jack, he jolted forward and altered his expression to one which was more attentive. Jack smiled to himself. Although it had been many years since his spell in uniform he still remembered when he'd done this and knew exactly what the officer was experiencing. This role, and that of prisoner sitting at hospital – which is what some poor sod would be doing at Mathew Alexander's bedside right now – were two of the most boring tasks in the job. Flashing his identity card, Jack rattled off his name and as the officer scribed his arrival onto the visitors log he offered a sympathetic smile. 'Don't worry another couple of hours and you'll be done,' Jack said walking away.

More tape woven between trees diverted him off the main track and piloted him into the woods. Immediately, he saw evidence of a vehicle having ploughed its way through here – tyre tracks had gouged undulating ruts into the soft earth, and flattened and ripped up undergrowth. Keeping to one side he carefully plodded on, watching where he placed his feet, and within a few minutes of tramping across uneven woodland vegetation he could hear voices. Seconds later, half a dozen white suited people came into view. They encircled the charred shell of a car – its distinct shape announcing the make as a mini. Jack picked out DI Harrison among the group and headed toward him.

As he neared several heads twisted around.

DI Harrison greeted him, 'Morning again Jack.' Then, chinning toward the burned out mini he said, 'It's definitely Carrie's. There's no number plates, but we've confirmed it from its chassis and engine number.'

'And Carrie?' Jack asked sidling next to his DI.

'The car's empty and so far no sign of her. Though we've got some marks going away from the car where it looks like someone's been dragged from it, and we've found a woman's shoe and Carrie's credit card just over there.' Dick Harrison flicked his head towards a line of bushes. 'We've placed yellow markers next to them and taken photo's in situ and I've just requested task force to turn out so that we can do a thorough search.' He locked eyes with Jack. 'It's not looking good for Carrie I'm afraid.'

27

'And you say Mathew's in hospital – he's been involved in a crash?' Jack stamped his feet on the ground. He could feel a chill getting through. He wished he had kept his overcoat on – it was colder than he anticipated.

DI Dick Harrison nodded, 'Last night. I've managed to speak with someone from Road Traffic this morning. They say it happened around nine. He was driving home from the Lamorna Wink and he lost his car on a bend not far from the pub. Crashed into a wall. Wrote the car off. He's apparently told the officers that someone ran him off the road, but there's only one set off skid marks at the scene, and they've spoken with the landlord who's given them a statement that Mathew had drunk a couple of pints and two double whiskies before he drove home. They've got a blood sample at the hospital so it'll probably show he was over the limit.'

'Badly injured?'

'A couple of cracked ribs and some cuts and bruises. He's very lucky. Especially given the state of his car.'

'Are they keeping him in?'

'At least twenty-four hours for observations.' The DI rubbed his hands. 'And that serves our purpose wonderfully. I want you to swear out a magistrates warrant and do a search of his house. I'll stay here and oversee this and I'll call out a forensic team and a couple from the office to join you at Matthew's place. I want you to go over that house with a fine tooth-comb. If you find anything let me know immediately and we meet back at the office for a six o'clock briefing this evening.'

The crack of branches behind them made Jack and the DI turn. Coming toward them was Fabi. The white forensic suit she was wearing was far too big and it hung in folds around her.

Jack couldn't help but smirk. He said, 'Afternoon DC Nosenzo, good of you to come.'

She blushed and for a moment her mouth fell open but she didn't speak. Then, recovering her composure replied, 'It's only half-nine. Sorry I'm late. I hadn't got a protective suit in my car. I had to call into the station on my way here.'

The DI said, 'Take no notice Fabi.' Shaking his head, he smiled. 'You'll have to get used to him you know. He's always like this. You're here now and that's the main thing.'

'Have I missed anything?' she asked.

Jack quickly filled her in and then added, 'And you and I young lady have got important work to do. We've got to swear out a warrant and then go to Mathew's place to carry out a proper search. Important evidence to find.'

'And before you go,' interposed the DI, 'Keep your head down at the cottage. I'm doing a press conference at two o'clock. The media have got wind about this so I'm going to have to put something out about our investigation into Carrie's disappearance. It should be on this evening's news and with a bit of luck it might help us find out a bit more about her.'

**

By lunchtime Renaissance Cottage and grounds had become a no-go zone. Although Mathew's place was a good quarter of a mile from his nearest neighbour a uniform constable was on sentry duty, guarding the entrance, particularly on the look-out for the press, while a forensic team had sealed off the entire cottage in preparation for a thorough examination.

Jack had telephoned DI Harrison, updating him, and got feedback that a search of the section of woodland where they had found Carrie's burned out car hadn't turned up her body, though they had found evidence of a shallow grave nearby and an excavation had just started. 'At least we've got something to wet the press's appetite,' the DI ended on an excited note.

Acting as Crime Scene Manager, with Fabi at his shoulder, Jack returned to his task, travelling from room to room, briefly watching the conduct of each of the forensic officers, checking on their progress. Each room had become a separate crime scene, being subjected to the same thorough examination. He knew it was going to be a laborious and time consuming job and an hour-in Jack took a break, leaving Fabi to oversee the work while he made his way outside to the rear garden. With his hands in his pockets he stared out beyond the adjoining fields to where the Atlantic met the sky. In the distance he watched dark brooding storm clouds patrolling the skies. It looked as though they were about to unleash their torrent any time soon. His thoughts started to darken like the sky. Without warning Claire's dead face burst into his skull. Closing his eyes, he tried to will away the vision. He'd thought that with the counselling, he had put the traumatic event of that evening behind him, but since the unearthing of Angel May's suicide Claire's death had become a recurring vision, replaying inside his head, but like a musical rallentando – haunting him.

A sudden and unexpected cry caused him to snap open his eyes, collapsing the mental picture, thankfully ridding him of the gruesome apparition. It was Fabi. In the kitchen.

She called, 'Jack, you need to see this ... they've found blood.'

28

'The grave was fresh but it had only just been started and not finished,' said DI Harrison, smoothing the front of his tie against his shirt as he took his seat at the conference table. Directly behind him, a white board had been set up, displaying a large crime scene photograph of the charred skeleton of Carrie Jefferies mini. Its front end was nose down in a ditch and it was surrounded by charcoal blackened trees and shrivelled bushes caused by the fireball from the car. There were also enlarged snaps of a dark blue ballet pump among dead leaves and a bank debit card lying on top of broken twigs. Her name could just be made out on the card. 'Operation Artist' was the official title given to the investigation and that headed up the board. Below that, Carrie's name had been underlined. Her date of birth was missing and her address was shown as Renaissance Cottage. And there still wasn't a photograph of her, though they now had a digital image compiled by Tammy and James Callaghan, who both said it was a good likeness. There was also a head and shoulders photo of Mathew Alexander with the word SUSPECT emblazoned beneath it in capital letters. 'It's hard to say if the grave is connected to the discovery of Carrie's car, and I am keeping an open mind, though for me, the proximity of a partially dug grave close to her burned out mini, where we've also found a number of small bloodstains, and the finding of her shoe and credit card, together with evidence that someone had been dragged through the undergrowth towards the grave, is too much of a coincidence.' Dick Harrison explored the faces of his team. 'So we have to ask ourselves why Carrie wasn't buried and left there. Did something happen to make the killer change his plan? Where is Carrie's body now? Has it been carried further into the woods and buried there?' The DI paused, 'With those questions unanswered, I've arranged for a search and rescue dog to be at the scene tomorrow. We're going to increase the cover of our search and I'm also bringing in another task force team to help. That estate is huge as you know and a lot of it is woodland.' Slapping his hands palm-flat on the table and centring his gaze on Jack he continued, 'Right Jack, I want you to tell us what you and Fabi have found at Mathew's place today.'

Jack eased himself back in his seat and gazed around the table. Clearing his throat, he said, 'Forensics found evidence of blood stains in the kitchen. It looks as though Mathew's tried to clean it up with bleach but fortunately for us he's not been thorough enough. They tell me that despite the contamination there might be enough to enable a DNA analysis, and they've recovered hair from a brush she used so they're going to fast-track it and see if it's a match to Carrie's. We should know within forty-eight hours. And they've also found particles of glass located in the kitchen. They've found the remnants of a couple of wineglasses in the bin outside. It looks as though someone threw the glasses and they've smashed over different parts of the kitchen floor.' Leaning forward, resting his arms on the table he added, 'And what is even more interesting is there is evidence of a recent fire at the bottom of the garden. It looks as though clothing has been burned. An accelerant was used so sadly forensics can't get anything from it.' Following a quick pause, he continued, 'But what we have got is a pair of muddy walking shoes, which were in a kitchen cupboard, and, as an added bonus we've also found a couple of wraps of coke in a drawer in Mathew's painting studio upstairs. There's other paraphernalia in there as well which suggests he's a regular user.'

The DI interjected, engaging looks with Jack, 'The shoes look promising, especially given that we've found Carrie's car in the woods. They've gone off for analysis?'

Jack nodded.

'And with regard to the drugs … haven't we heard evidence of that already? Didn't he use when he was with his model girlfriend, Angel May?'

'Yes Boss. Emma Kirby gave us that information. She said that it was Mathew who got Angel into using the stuff.'

Dick Harrison flipped his gaze from one detective to another, 'Very interesting don't you think? It seems like Mathew Alexander has got quite a few questions to answer.' Looking at Jack he added, 'And on that note I want you and Fabi to begin with that tomorrow. I've spoken with the hospital and they tell me they can discharge him in the morning. He's got a couple of cracked ribs but that doesn't stop us talking to him. I want you and Fabi to check what time he's being released and arrest him and bring him back for interview. The rest of us, we have our work cut out. Time is no longer on our side. It's now eleven days since Carrie went missing. Mathew's cottage is in a relatively quiet location, though he does have to pass a few houses to get to the woods at Boskenna, so I want house-to-house at every possible route he could have taken to get there. Did anyone see Carrie's mini during the time she went missing? And we visit the Callaghans again. I want more background about Carrie and Mathew, if they can provide it – every facet of their relationship and I want to know the ins-and-outs of every argument they've witnessed between the pair. And get back on to the Australian authorities. Press them about Carrie. Tell them that this is now a murder enquiry. We need to find out as much as we can about her.' Pausing, he slowly gazed around, 'And before I wind this up I want the suicide of Angel May re-visited. Get back onto the DC who dealt with the job and get the full forensic and pathology reports from her post mortem. The more I hear about Mathew Alexander the more it concerns me.'

29

Slipping down his headphones Mathew Alexander eased himself up in his hospital bed. He grimaced, biting down on his bottom lip. The slightest movement hurt like hell. Pulling his gaze away from his bedside TV he looked over to where the uniform police officer was seated by the door; he had woken up to find him there and he instantly concluded he wasn't there to protect him.

He's there to make sure I don't escape.

Noisily he cleared his throat and tried to get eye-contact but the young officer immediately shied away his gaze. That frustrated him. The officer had been doing this repeatedly all morning and when he'd tried to engage in dialogue he had fared no better with the response from him. All the young man had kept telling him was that he'd been instructed to stay there and not get involved in any form of conversation.

Bringing his notice back to the television the on-screen image grabbed his attention and, with a sense of urgency, he slid on the headphones. The picture of the burned out mini that had been on screen a second earlier was replaced by a man in a suit standing outside a police station. The strap-line running along the bottom announced that it was Detective Inspector Dick Harrison, Devon & Cornwall Police.

He listened to him saying, 'Carrie Jefferies, a thirty-three-year-old woman, who we believe originates from Australia but is currently living near Boskenna, was reported missing on the twenty-sixth of April. There have been no confirmed sightings of Carrie for eleven days and, as far as we can establish, she has not made any attempt to contact anyone. Earlier today we found her burned out car in the woods at Boskenna and we currently have teams of officers searching that area. We are also searching premises where she's been living for the past year. We are extremely concerned for her welfare and we are urging anyone who knows Carrie, or anyone who has had any contact with her, or might know anything as to her whereabouts to contact us immediately.'

As the detective finished speaking his name was replaced by a telephone number which travelled slowly along the bottom of the TV.

Mathew pulled off his headphones. He could feel trickles of sweat running down each side of his ribcage. As he glanced over to where the officer was seated one thought occupied his mind – they were coming to arrest him!

30

In the interview room at Penzance police station Jack examined Mathew Tobias Alexander's face across the desk. The entire right and hand side was swollen and covered in purple bruising and his eye was partially closed. Jack thought he looked more the prize fighter than the artist, though he had no sympathy for him. As far as he was concerned he had got his just deserts. In fact, he was hoping that by the end of the day he would be heaping a whole lot more pain on his aching frame, if this interview went according to plan.

Fabi opened the proceedings by reminding Mathew that he was under caution and informed him that the interview was being videoed. As she talked, the duty solicitor representing Mathew scribbled a note.

Mathew replied, 'You're way off beam you know that don't you?' The edges of his mouth curled up as he talked and he shuffled uneasily on his seat. The look he bore was one of discomfort.

Raising his eyebrows Jack fixed Mathew with a questioning stare, 'You look uncomfortable there Mathew. Are you okay?'

'It's just my ribs. It hurts when I talk. In fact, it hurts when I do anything.'

'Well if things get unbearable for you let us know and we'll stop, but in the meantime as you've been discharged from the hospital we'll continue with this interview.' Trying to hide the sarcasm in his voice Jack leaned forward and rested his elbows on the table. 'That comment you've just made. Why do you say that Mathew?'

'Well first of all how do you know Carrie's dead? Have you found her body?'

'Are you expecting us to find a body?'

Mathew's expression changed to one of shock-horror, 'No. You've got this all wrong I haven't done anything to Carrie. I wouldn't hurt Carrie for the world. It wasn't me who did that to her mini. You need to be looking for someone else for this.'

'Who should we be looking for then?'

'Well trying to find whoever ran me off the road would be a good start. They could have killed me. It could be the same person.'

'And who do you think that might be? Have you an idea?'

He shrugged his shoulders. 'I don't know, do I? That's your job isn't it? You should be trying to find that out instead of dragging in an innocent man from his hospital bed.'

'I can assure you your accident is being investigated as we speak, and as for being dragged out of your hospital bed, you were discharged this lunchtime. You are here Mathew, because we're trying to find out what's happened to Carrie.'

'And that's what I'd like to find out.'

'Good we're singing from the same hymn sheet then. Now can I just take you back to when you last saw Carrie. Sunday the twenty-sixth.'

'What about it?'

'Well, earlier you had an argument didn't you at the Callaghan's where you were having a meal?'

Mathew offered back a nonchalant look.

'Tell us about it. How it started.'

'I can't remember how it started I'd had a fair bit to drink. I've been under a bit of pressure of late and things just got on top of me. When they do I just snap. I know it was my fault. I've apologised to James and Tammy about it.'

'Do you remember what it was about?'

'Not really. It wasn't much. I just lost my cool and had a go at Carrie. I regret it now.'

Jack decided not to press at this stage. He said, 'We're told that Carrie drove you home from the Callaghan's'

Mathew nodded.

'Did you go straight home?'

For a moment he seemed to think about the question, then, he answered, 'Yes I think so. I was fairly blasted by that time. Yes, I'm sure Carrie drove straight home. I can't remember stopping anywhere if that's what you mean.'

'And what about when you got home?'

'What do you mean?'

'Did the argument continue?'

'I don't remember much. As I say, I'd had a fair bit to drink. To be honest I was pissed.'

'Who threw the glass?'

Mathew's mouth dropped open and he was quiet for a brief spell. Then, he replied, 'What glass?'

'We found the remains of two wineglasses in your bin. And we also found fragments on your kitchen floor.'

'I don't remember. I was smashed out of my skull. I've already told you.' There was a strain of tension in his response.

'Is this getting to you Mathew? I detect a little agitation in your tone.'

He exerted himself, screwing up his face before answering, 'Agitation? I'm fucking angry! And so would you be if you were sat in my place. I get dragged out of my hospital bed with three busted ribs and told I'm being arrested for murder. How would you react?'

'We've already clarified this Mathew you weren't dragged out of bed. The doctor discharged you.'

'You know what I fucking mean.'

'Please don't swear Mathew. I'm not swearing at you.'

For a moment Mathew locked eyes. Then, taking a deep breath he replied, 'Sorry.'

'Apology accepted. Now let's get to the matter in hand. Just putting aside the broken glasses for a moment. Did you carry on arguing when you got home?'

'I don't remember. I've told you I was drunk.'

'What do you remember?'

'Nothing much about that night. I woke up just before eleven the next morning and Carrie had gone.'

'When you say gone? ... '

'She hadn't slept in the bed. She hadn't slept in the spare room. When I got up the front and back doors were unlocked, her car had gone and she'd taken her handbag with all her personal stuff. That's it.'

'And did you try to contact her?'

'Yes. I rung her mobile several times and she didn't answer. And I rang James to see if she'd gone there.'

'Did you have any concerns?'

'Concerns?'

'Yes, that something might have happened to her?'

'No, not really. I thought she'd gone off in a huff because of our argument.'

'But you just said you don't remember much about the argument. Now you say you thought she'd gone off in a huff because of it, so it must have been pretty bad between you.'

'Look we rowed at James and Tammy's. I know I said some nasty things to her that I'm not proud of now, but what I mean is that after we'd got home I don't remember anything at all.'

'And you don't remember anything about the broken glasses?'

He shook his head, 'No.'

'And what about the blood?'

Mathew flashed a hesitant look, 'Blood?'

'Yes the blood in the kitchen that you tried to clean up?'

On that note the duty solicitor shot up his head from his notebook, quickly glancing sideways at Mathew. Then, he set his eyes on Jack. 'Detectives I'd like to stop the interview there. I need to speak with my client.'

31

Upstairs in the CID office Jack was sitting at his desk, one leg up, calf resting along the edge. Two-handed he held a mug full of steaming tea and a beaming smile lit up his face. Opposite, at her desk, Fabi had her head down, going through her pre-interview notes.

'That looks like a victorious grin Jack,' said DI Harrison appearing from his office.

'Just hit Mathew with the broken glass and the blood evidence. You should have seen his face.'

'A picture?'

'A bloody Mona Lisa. He's now having a scrum-down with his brief. He stopped the interview unfortunately'

'You're going back down?'

'I'm giving them twenty minutes and then Fabi and I are going down for the kill.'

As Jack went to take a drink of his tea his desk phone rang.

***

Jack lowered himself into the seat across from Mathew Alexander, trying to catch his eyes but Mathew avoided him, glancing down at the table. Jack smiled to himself as he shuffled into a comfortable position.

The duty solicitor was the first to speak. 'My client would like to make a statement.'

Jack interlocked his fingers and cracked back his knuckles. 'That's fine, but we would like to ask him more questions.' He glanced at Fabi and gave a slight nod.

She started the recording machine and reminded Mathew he was still under caution.

Jack released his fingers and placed his hands palm flat. 'Mathew when we finished our last interview I was about to ask you about the blood we found in your kitchen. Would you now like to explain that?'

'Look I panicked about that, that's why I didn't tell you. I've spoken with my solicitor and I want to tell you the truth.'

'That would be appreciated.'

'The honest answer is I don't know how the two glasses got broken, or how the blood got there, although some of it was mine – I stood on the broken glass in my bare feet. I cut the bottom of my foot.'

'You say some of it?'

'Yes there was a small pool near the fridge door. It had dried up. It wasn't mine I checked.'

'So it was Carrie's?'

He shrugged his shoulders, 'I don't know. Like I say I don't remember. I've already told you I'd had a fair bit to drink that night.'

'What you are telling me is that you can remember being driven home but you can't remember anything after that. The crucial bits about the broken glass or how blood got on to the kitchen floor.'

'It's exactly that. Honestly. I can't even remember going to bed. My mind's a complete blank. I was pissed. I think we argued when we got home but I genuinely can't remember. I just remember getting up the next morning and Carrie had gone. Taken her bag and the car – like I told you.'

'So why didn't you say that when I first raised it? And why did you clean up the blood with bleach?'

He was quiet for a few seconds, then, he answered, 'I told you I panicked. The broken glass, the blood and we'd argued that night beforehand. I knew it would look suspicious.'

'Okay, just putting that to one side, tell me what your actions were after you found Carrie had gone?'

'Well, like I say, at first I just thought she'd gone off in a huff and I tried ringing her but she didn't answer, so I rang James to see if she'd gone there but he told me they'd not seen her. Then, because of the blood I rang the hospital just in case she'd had an accident. You can check.'

'Why didn't you ring the police?'

'I don't know. I just didn't.'

'I asked you earlier if you were concerned about Carrie and you said you weren't. Now you're telling me you rang the hospital.'

'That's different. I wasn't concerned that anything had happened to her, as in missing, or dead, or anything like that what you're suggesting, but I thought she might have cut herself with the broken glass.'

'Do you think she's dead Mathew?'

For a moment Mathew stared across the table, then, he took a sharp intake of breath and said, 'You obviously think she is. And you obviously think I did it, otherwise you wouldn't have arrested me.'

'You know we found her burned out mini don't you?'

'Yes in the woods not far from here. I saw it on the news.'

'And we also found items belonging to Carrie nearby.'

'Have you found her then?'

'Do you think we might do?'

'You're trying to put words in my mouth.' He slammed his hands onto the table. 'Look I haven't done anything to Carrie.'

'We found some drag marks leading away from the car and it looks as though someone has started digging a grave. Now would you think that whoever did that would be covered in dirt?' As he finished speaking Jack thought he caught something in Mathew's eyes but he blinked it quickly away.

Mathew was silent for a few seconds before replying, 'Maybe.' Gulping, he added, 'I don't know.'

'Well I would have thought so. Conditions in that wood are not good. I was down there this morning and I got caked in mud.'

Mathew shrugged and gave Jack a 'what's that to do with me' look.

'What I'm getting at Mathew is that this morning we got a warrant and carried out a search of your home and found a pair of walking shoes in a cupboard in your kitchen and they're covered in dried mud. And while you were in conference with your solicitor I got a phone call informing me that they've found a spade in the boot of your car with dried mud on it. Do you think when we do tests on those that the mud on those boots and the spade will match that in the woods near where we found Carrie's burned out car and the shallow grave?'

Mathew's jaw dropped. 'This is a fucking stitch-up. Someone's trying to frame me.'

'And at the bottom of your garden we found the remains of a fire, where clothing has been found burned. Forensics are checking to see if there are any labels to identify the clothing. But, do you know what Mathew, I think we'll find that it's your clothing. Am I right?'

Mathew jerked upright, shooting a quick glance at his solicitor, 'Someone's trying to frame me. I haven't done anything.' Returning his gaze to Jack he added, 'Look, I found my clothes muddy like that the morning I woke up and Carrie had gone. I don't know how they got like that. I must have fallen down or something. I've told you I was well and truly pissed that night.'

'Why did you burn them? Why not just wash them?'

'I don't know.' He paused a moment and then said, 'Again, I just panicked.'

'The other simple explanation is that you tried to destroy the evidence. I think your clothes got like that after you drove Carrie's car to the woods that night, because you'd killed her at home, and you started to dig a grave for her, but then something or someone disturbed you.'

'I never went to the woods.'

'You just said you don't remember what you did. You were drunk.'

'I'd have remembered that.'

'Is she in the woods Mathew? Have you buried Carrie in the woods?'

'Read my lips. I – never – went – to – the- woods. Why don't you believe me?'

'Well let's look at things from my perspective. You were the last person to see Carrie. You argued that night. We've found evidence of broken glass and blood in your kitchen, which you've tried to clean up – with bleach. We've found her car dumped in the woods less than a mile from your home, items that belonged to Carrie and a grave that's been dug nearby. And, at your home we've found muddy boots, and a spade in the boot of your car with mud on it and you've admitted burning your clothes because they were covered in mud. Isn't that a big enough picture for you? The vast majority of people are killed by someone they know.'

He pushed himself back, 'I'm saying nothing else. If you think I killed Carrie, then you go ahead and prove it.'

32

Jack was alone in the office, seated at his desk with his head resting in his hands, re-playing the events of that day in his thoughts. Everyone else had gone home, or to the pub, following the break-up of evening briefing half an hour ago. He had lied when he told those who were off to the pub that he had some paperwork to tidy up and then he would join them. The truth was he wasn't in the mood. He was drained. The case had taken more out of him than he had thought and made him realise that he'd done far too much too quickly after his six-month layoff. Also, and he was reluctant to admit it, he knew that his age was a big factor on his weariness. Time was when he'd leave briefing, trot off to the pub with his colleagues, down four or five pints, go home and have supper and be up before 7a.m. the next morning, fired up for another 14-hour day.

You're getting old Jack Buchan. Too old for this game. Maybe it's time to retire.

He shifted his gaze from the neat pile of interview notes in front of him to the incident board at the front of the office. He looked at the head and shoulders photograph of Mathew Tobias Alexander. He and Fabi had reached an impasse with him. Mathew no longer wanted to answer their questions and they had lodged him back in a cell. They only had another sixteen hours to break him or come up with the damning evidence to charge him otherwise he was out on bail.

At that evening's briefing, DI Harrison told them that a good proportion of the woods had been searched but they still hadn't found any further sign of Carrie. They had found and dug up a couple of graves but these had only held dog carcasses; more than likely someone's pet. Another task force unit was joining the team tomorrow to double their search capacity. At Mathew's house they had found no other sign of blood and his car had been put onto a low-loader and taken away for forensic examination. House-to-house enquiries with the occupants of the few cottages on the route from his home to Boskenna had not turned up anything and there were no roadside cameras in the location to log Mathew's movement in his or Carrie's car. Regarding his involvement in the suicide of his former girlfriend, Angel May, two officers were still ploughing through the weighty inquest file, trying to determine if there were any fresh lines of enquiry. So far they had drawn a blank. He and Fabi were still tasked with interviewing him about that but at the moment that was more of a fishing exercise without a new element of approach. Jack brought back his attention to his neat paperwork and let off a long sigh. It looked like they were going to have no option but to release him.

Unless...

He suddenly remembered his and Fabi's conversation with Pippa from the gallery. Of course, Mathew had drugged her and raped her, hadn't he? And although she had told them all she wanted to do was put it behind her he was sure that with Fabi's help they could persuade her to make a statement against him. Especially if she learned that he could be getting away with murder. He was certain that would prick her conscience. At least it would give them a holding charge while they carried out all their enquiries.

I'll air that at tomorrow morning's briefing.

With renewed vigour he pushed himself up, picked up his papers, tapped the edges straight and placed them in his top tray. He was about to lift his coat from the back of his chair when his desk phone rang. He looked at the clock on the wall. 8.50p.m. He wondered if it was one of the team ringing him up to see how long he would be before he joined them. For a moment he was going to ignore it; he couldn't face them tonight. And then he thought about the call Emma Kirby had made several nights ago and in that instant he made the decision to snatch it up.

'DC Buchan, Penzance CID.'

There was no response. He strained his ears and picked up the sound of soft breathing on the other end. After a good few seconds he said, 'DC Jack Buchan, if you have a problem I can help. If you have any information regarding the disappearance of Carrie Jefferies, I can take it down. You don't have to leave your name if you don't want to.'

There was a couple more seconds of silence and then a slight voice said, 'I'm sorry to disturb you. I don't know if I'm speaking out of turn and I don't want to get anyone into trouble.'

It was female. Jack tried to visualise the caller. He thought she sounded to be in her late twenties, early thirties. The accent, although local, had an edge of refinement. He replied, 'Anything you tell me will be in complete confidence, I promise.'

There was a moment's pause again and then the woman said, 'I've been told you've arrested Mathew Alexander over his girlfriend going missing?'

Jack's ears pricked up. He responded, 'We have a man in custody regarding the disappearance of Carrie Jefferies, yes. Do you have some information about that?'

At first she stuttered over her words, but then she blurted out, 'Not about that I haven't, but I have about what he did to Tammy Callaghan. Has she told you about the time he tried to rape her?'

33

Jack finally gave up trying to get to sleep shortly after 5a.m., got up, dressed in a pair of jeans and sweatshirt and, donning his fleece and waterproof, took Mollie out for a brisk early morning walk. He strolled for over an hour across fields watching her disappearing in and out of hedgerows as she searched for game while he pondered on the message delivered by the previous evening's mysterious caller; the investigation was certainly throwing up some interesting elements.

Back home he fed and watered Mollie, made himself a hot drink and some toast, and then showered and changed into his work clothes. Checking his watch as he locked his front door he noted that dawn was still a good half hour away as he set off for the station.

Not surprisingly he was first in the office, and with nothing to do but wait, he made another drink of tea and strolled back and forth around the office, his gaze constantly going to the incident board.

At 7.30a.m. Fabi entered the room and Jack made a bee-line for her.

Looking at his watch as if she was late he said excitedly, 'I've been waiting for you.'

Dumping her bag on the desk she replied, 'Why what's up?'

'I got a phone call last night while you were all out at the pub.' He told her about the information the female caller had given him.'

Fabi threw him an astonished look, 'Wow.'

'Exactly.'

'What are you wanting to do?'

'I'm just waiting for the DI to come in, then I'm going to tell him. And then you and I are going to pay her a visit. James is likely to be there so we need to get him out of the house. I'd rather speak with her alone if we can.'

Jack rapped loudly on the front door of the old fisherman's cottage at Penberth and in less than half a minute Tammy Callaghan was at the door. He watched her face as she offered up a surprised expression.

'Oh, I thought you'd arranged to meet James at the station to check through his statement. He set off five minutes ago.'

'Yes I know we watched him leave.'

Tammy's face morphed into a look of puzzlement. 'I don't understand.'

'I arranged it so it would be like this. It's you we want to talk to.'

Her eyebrows pinched together. 'Me?'

'It's about your attack Mrs Callaghan,' said Fabi.

She said the words 'My attack.' but there was no element of question behind them and Jack immediately knew that last night's phone call had not been mischievous.

'Can we come in?' Jack deliberately placed his foot on the threshold knowing that her reaction would be to take a step back. It worked, leaving him a gap to take another step forward and in two steps he was inside her home. Fabi followed, closing the door quietly behind them.

The front door gave them immediate access to a small low-ceiling lounge, the feature of which was an open stone fireplace with a log-burner. From a long mullion window strong sunshine filled the room, its rays highlighting thousands of dust motes floating gently around. The only furnishings were a two-seater sofa, an armchair, a bookcase, crammed with books and flat screen TV. Anything else would have made the room look crowded. It reminded Jack of his own lounge.

Tammy turned her back to them and, calling back over her shoulder, said, 'We can talk through here,' and walked out of the lounge to the back of the house.

They stepped through a small kitchen-diner, which was fitted with a mishmash of furnishings and units that was in the shabby chic style – more DIY than bespoke – and into a south-facing conservatory, kitted out with rattan chairs covered with tartan throws and cushions.

With extended arm Tammy offered them a seat. As she sat down in a chair she said, 'How did you find out about the attack? Has Mathew confessed?'

Jack responded, 'I'm afraid I'm not at liberty to say how we came by the information Tammy, you have to understand that. Safe to say we obviously know about it and we'd like your take on what happened.'

'Will James get to know?'

'You haven't told him?' said Fabi. She had taken out her notebook and pen from her bag and was fanning through the pages to find a blank one.

'I didn't know how to. He's friends with Mathew. After that last time I thought that'd be an end to it so decided not to tell him.'

Jack leaned forward, clasping his hands and resting his lower arms along his thighs. 'Look Tammy, Mathew is in a heap of trouble. It's going to come out sooner rather than later, we found blood at his home, which we think is Carrie's and you'll have seen on the news that we've found her car burned out in the woods at Boskenna.'

She put a hand to mouth, 'Oh God. Have you found Carrie? Is she dead?'

'We're searching the woods as we speak. I think it will only be a matter of time before we found her body.'

'I knew Mathew had got a nasty streak in him but I never thought he'd do this.'

'He attacked you Tammy. That show's how nasty he can be.'

She nodded.

'It would help if you told us about it.'

Tammy brushed her hands down the front of her jeans, then glimpsed at them. 'God I'm shaking.'

Fabi said, 'I know this must be awful for you Tammy, but if I tell you that you're not the first person he's attacked like this, maybe you'll realise why we're talking to you this morning. Mathew is a nasty piece of work and the sooner he's behind bars the better.'

Following a short pause, during which she alternated her gaze between Fabi and Jack, she replied, 'He didn't actually...' she took a deep breath '... you know, rape me. I managed to stop him.' She paused again. 'I threatened to stab him with one of my kitchen knives. Will I get into trouble?'

Fabi gave her a sympathetic smile, 'You were protecting yourself Tammy. No you won't get into trouble. Do you feel able to tell us what Mathew did to you?'

'To be honest it all started innocently. I've tried reflecting on it and wondered if I'm somehow to blame for what he did.'

'You are not in any way responsible for what Mathew did. You mustn't think that at all. Mathew did what he did because he wanted to. End of.' There was a raised inflection in Fabi's voice.

'I know deep down I didn't do anything wrong, but I shouldn't have let it go on like I did before I did something about it. I know I should have told James. I should have reported him to you.'

'You handled it how you thought best at the time.' Fabi held Tammy's gaze. 'Would you like to go through it? Tell us how it started and what he did.'

She let out a deep breath and put a hand to her chest, 'It started with just a bit of fun about six months ago. They came round for a few drinks, him and Carrie, and half way through the evening Mathew followed me into the kitchen when I went to get some more wine. We just got chatting and had a bit of a laugh and Mathew helped me open the wine. I couldn't get the cork out. He sort of held my wrist and helped me. I didn't think anything of it until the next time they came round when we invited them for a meal. He started getting a bit close then, brushing past me and because I'd not had as much to drink I noticed it. As the night wore on he got a bit closer, and then as they left he gave me a hug and kissed me on the cheek, which I felt uncomfortable about. The third time he started flirting with me. He followed me into the kitchen again when I went for the wine and told me that I'd got a great figure and that he'd love to paint me. I told him straight that if anyone was going to paint me it would be James. He just laughed and played it down by saying it was a joke.' She swung her gaze back and forth between the two detectives. 'But it wasn't. I knew he was being serious. And then after that, that's when he attacked me.'

'When was this?' asked Fabi.

She stared over Fabi's head, through the conservatory windows and for a few seconds held it there. Then, pulling back her eyes answered, 'Three months ago now. He turned up just before lunchtime when James had gone off to take his work to the gallery. He said that he and Carrie had just had a row and he'd come away for some breathing space. I made him a coffee, and he told me that they weren't getting on and that he felt she was using him for his money. I just listened. When he'd drunk his coffee, he thanked me for listening, and said what good friends we'd been to him, and that he didn't know where he'd be without us, and as he was putting his mug in the sink he just grabbed hold of me, and pulled me to him and kissed me on the lips. It was such a shock. I pushed him away and told him that he should go and I made an excuse that James would be home soon. Mathew just laughed and said he knew James would be gone for most of the day and he just grabbed me again. Around the waist, really tight, and said he knew that I wanted him and he grabbed hold of my backside and started kissing my neck. That's when I grabbed the knife off the side.'

Fabi stopped making notes and said, 'What did you do?'

'I didn't stab him if that's what you mean? I managed to pull myself free and just held it there, waving it at his face. I swore at him and told him to get out. The cheeky bastard just laughed at me again and said that I didn't know what I was missing and then he left as if nothing had happened.'

'And you said you never told James about this?' interjected Jack.

Tammy shook her head. 'I didn't know how to tell him. I mean should I mention the flirting bit? I was worried James might think I encouraged him.'

'That's nonsense Tammy.' Fabi responded.

She locked onto Fabi's eyes. 'I just keep going through things in my head. Was it my fault? Did I lead him on?' She started to cry.

Fabi closed her notebook, left her chair and reached down and touched Tammy's hands, 'No you did not. This is Mathew's fault not yours. He should pay for this.' Lowering her voice, she added, 'It's time to make a statement Tammy.'

34

Mathew woke with a jolt. Something had caused it. Confused he quickly scoured the room, holding his breath. Nothing. For a few seconds he lay there listening. He remembered what had happened the last time and he was instantly drawn to the window where the curtains were open and where strong moonlight bled into the room bathing everything in an eerie half-light.

For a moment he couldn't move. His stomach emptied and he could feel himself start to panic. He knew he would have to get a hold of himself and took a deep breath. A sharp pain shot through his ribcage like an electric shock reminding him of his busted ribs, making him feel sick. Steadying his breathing he waited for the pain to subside, then gently pulling aside his duvet he slipped out of bed and made for the window, his face close to the glass. The pane instantly misted over – an opaque veil blocked his view. Stepping back, it cleared within seconds, and he started his search of the garden below, swinging his gaze out to the sycamore where his tormentor had appeared previously. A sudden movement caught his eye – something stepped out from behind the trunk into the clearing. It was the spectre again, silhouetted against the moonlight. He stiffened as a bolt of nervous energy travelled through his body. For a moment he held his breath, watching whoever it was stare back at him. Then, he started to shake. He could feel a panic attack coming on and he started to hyperventilate. As light-headedness started to overwhelm him the phone rang behind, making him jump and jerking his thoughts back to the moment. Spinning around to the bedside cabinet he snatched the handset out of its holder, hit the answer button and angrily shouted, 'What the fuck do you want?'

For a couple of seconds there was no response. He could feel his heart lurching against his chest. Then, a loud crackling sound buzzed down the line forcing him to pull it away from his ear. He looked at the handset for a moment and then returned it to his ear just as a muffled voice said, 'You're gonna get what's coming to you.'

35

In the witness room of Truro Crown Court Jack was sitting at a table drumming a repetitive tattoo on its surface with his fingers. Feelings of anxiousness and frustration were coursing through him and he tried to unfasten the knot that gripped his stomach. He knew why he was in this state. It had taken four months for Mathew Alexander's case to finally come before the courts and, even though the trial had opened two days ago, the jury still hadn't been sworn in and open addresses made. The prosecution and defence barristers were still locked in battle with the judge, arguing what evidence could be presented and if witnesses should be provided special measures. Jack hated this part of the judicial system: The legal games defence played at the expense of justice. Yesterday, Defence Counsel had already managed to get the Angel May suicide details thrown out. Jack, together with CPS had argued that this was part of the evidence which should be presented as bad character reference against Mathew but the judge had ruled in favour of the defence and dismissed it. Defence had also tried to get the murder charge dismissed on the grounds that they hadn't found Carrie's body and therefore the evidence was circumstantial. Thankfully prosecution had won that one. The defence barrister was now arguing that Tammy's evidence, with regard to the attack on her, and Mathew's rape of Pippa should be dealt with as separate issues in a separate trial. Jack prayed to God that this wouldn't happen. It highlighted just how bad Mathew was and what he was capable of.

Jack stopped drumming, took a deep breath and drifted his eyes to the far corner of the room where Fabi was in conversation with the female court usher. He couldn't overhear the conversation going on between them but he could see Fabi laughing. She looks relaxed, he thought, which surprised him. He knew from talking with her that this had been her biggest case to date and yet he had seen her work through it effortlessly – unfazed by its magnitude.

She'll make a good detective he thought.

The door to the courtroom suddenly opened, breaking his thoughts, and he swivelled round. Kate Carty, the prosecution barrister, stepped into the room wearing an expression that was purposeful and business-like.

Jack rose from his chair. His knees cracked.

Kate pulled her robes round her and broke into a half-smile. 'We had a good day today DC Buchan. The judge has ruled in our favour that we can present the evidence of Tammy Callaghan, though he has advised we would have a stronger case if we were to drop the indecency and reduce it to assault, and he has also agreed that Pippa Johnson's rape should remain as a charge, and in the case of both women he has agreed that they can give evidence behind a screen and he has warned defence about aggressive questioning. So, starting tomorrow we have a trial on our hands.

36

For three weeks and two days Jack and Fabi turned up every day to Truro Crown Court, listening to the evidence unfold. Kate Carty's presentation was clipped and to the point and she even threw in some levity which, Jack saw, pleased the jury. Tammy and Pippa had gone into the witness box and delivered their evidence nervously, but both had stuck to their statements. Pippa, especially, had come over well; the jury had sympathised with her. When she had finished he saw a couple of the female jurors looking towards Mathew in the dock and shoot him daggers.

The forensic specialist, a man in his late forties, with 23 years' experience, had given a laboured, yet polished performance, explaining carefully how each piece of evidence had been collected, stored and then examined. He presented first the bloodstains found in Mathew's kitchen, making special emphasis about how bleach had been used in an effort to conceal it. He also talked about how they had discovered a pair of walking boots in a cupboard, covered in dried mud, and how they had also recovered a spade in the boot of Mathew's car also encrusted in mud, and explained how both had been subjected to particle analysis and it was found that the samples matched those taken from the scene where Carrie's car had been found. The final part of his testimony was the discovery of small samples of blood close to the burned out mini. Defence argued that forensically they could not prove that the blood belonged to Carrie, because they had no body and so therefore no way of cross-matching. The specialist agreed on this point, but parried that they had taken hair samples from a brush Carrie had used at Mathew's house and recovered DNA from her toothbrush and these were an identical match to the blood found in Mathew's kitchen and in Boskenna Wood. The defence barrister had difficulty in hiding his disappointment as he flapped his gown around him, responded with, 'I have no more questions' and sat down.

Then it was Jack's turn to go into the witness box. As he held up the bible and swore on oath his head was already switching into a higher gear. He had done this dozens and dozens of times, and although the nerves were no longer there in terms of how he delivered his evidence they still existed with regard to the head-to-head with defence counsel. He always tried to tell himself that this was good. It kept him on his toes, though he never enjoyed it. On each and every occasion, whenever he'd walked out of the witness box, whether he had been in for ten minutes or several hours, he came away as drained as if he had been in a toe-to-toe fight and with a thundering headache. He knew this was going to be no different.

And yet, when he stepped out of the box three quarters of an hour later, he was surprised as to how humane the defence barrister had been with him. Though his evidence was not contested – it was all recorded – and though he had an answer for every question, he had constantly been guarded – expecting a counter-punch to be thrown in like a hand grenade – and yet none had come. For the first time, as the judge thanked him and he sat down at the back of the court, he didn't feel sick and exhausted.

Mathew didn't fare the same. Kate Carty was vicious. She never raised her voice or made a personal attack, though the questions she threw at him were as sharp and secure as a nail from a nail-gun. 'You like throwing your weight around don't you Mathew?' she arrowed at him after questioning him as to how he had treated Tammy. When he responded with a 'no', that was when she hit him with Pippa's rape – how he had drugged her and abused her, and how he had threatened her when she had challenged him. That was when Mathew lost his temper.

Banging his fist against the edge of the box he yelled, 'I can see what you're trying to do here.'

Calmly she said, 'What's that Mathew?'

'You're trying to make out that all this is my fault. That I was to blame for what happened to Tammy and Pippa and therefore I must have done something to Carrie.'

'Well did you?'

He speared a finger, 'No I fucking did not.'

The judge intervened quickly, telling Mathew that if he continued in this manner he would be removed from the court.

As the judge finished his warning Kate gripped the edges of her lapels, fought back a smirk and then delivered, 'And now that you've raised it let's talk about Carrie.'

For the next hour she asked him about his relationship with Carrie. Mathew agreed that it could be volatile at times and that when in drink he did get angry and verbally abusive, though he was adamant he had never assaulted her. Kate pushed him on this and for the first time Mathew broke down in tears.

'I may have done those other things,' he choked, 'And I'm sorry. I'm sorry to Tammy and to Pippa. I can see now how it's affected them. But as God is my judge, I have not killed Carrie.'

37

'Ladies and Gentlemen this is now your time,' the judge began. Resting on his elbows and entwining his fingers he leaned forward from his high position at the front of the court and looked down at the jury.

Jack watched him from the back of the courtroom, an anxious energy surging through him. He recollected how yesterday's hearing had finished with Mathew apologising for what he had done to Tammy and Pippa. And whilst it wasn't an admission of guilt he saw from the reaction on some of the juror's faces that they had viewed it as such. Now the judge was doing what he himself had been doing almost every day of this trial – studying each of the juror's faces.

The judge continued with his summation, 'I thank you for your patience. This has not been an easy case. Not easy because, although the defendant has been charged with murder, in this case no body has been found. It has also been complicated by the fact that we have heard very little about what type of person Carrie Jefferies was. We know very little about her life or her background, which is unusual, though we have been told roughly how old she was and that we believe she comes from Australia. But just because we know very little about someone does not mean a person cannot be charged with their murder, because we have heard from each of the witnesses something about the type of person Carrie Jefferies was. And they were able to do that because they have seen her, and they have talked with her and they have shared moments with her, so we know that Carrie Jefferies is indeed a living person and that up until the twenty-sixth of April this year she was very much alive...' He paused and then said, 'Until she disappeared that Sunday morning, and since then nothing has been heard from her.' He went on to talk about the evidence Tammy Callaghan had given prior to Carrie going missing and went on to remind the jury what the forensic specialist had offered up in his findings. Finally, he presented a summation of the other charges of the rape of Pippa and the common assault upon Tammy. Finishing, the judge said, 'When I release you shortly it will be your job to make a judgement based only on the facts that you have heard in this court. You must not be influenced by outside information and your role is to bring back a decision by which you all agree.'

***

Jack tried to catch the eyes of as many of the jurors as he could as they filed out of the courtroom to see if he could read anything into the looks they displayed which might give away the verdict they favoured. Many of them returned a deadpan expression leaving him with a feeling of frustration.

He decided to go for a stroll, and he wanted to be alone, so he told Fabi he had something he needed to take care of and that he'd see her after lunch when the courts reconvened. As she headed towards the canteen, he went off into town, deep in thought, mingling among the shoppers and the tourists as they ambled around in the July sunshine. He bought a daily paper from a newsagent's and grabbed a Cornish pasty from a high street bakers and ate it on the hoof out of its wrapper. Twenty minutes later, as he made his way back to the court house, he could feel a burning sensation erupting in his stomach as the pasty began repeating itself.

In the foyer of the court building he went through the airport style security check-in and joined Fabi in the witness room. She was sat at a table nursing a compressed cardboard cup of coffee. Looking up she asked, 'Did you get sorted what you needed to do?'

He didn't reply, but nodded and joined her.

For the next two hours they sat across from one another but didn't talk. Jack skip-read the newspaper he had bought while Fabi played with her phone. Occasionally Jack looked up to see her scrolling through Facebook, wondering what on earth people got from it. It amazed him how many of the team spent the beginning of the day talking about what they'd seen or shared on the social media site the previous evening. No one talks football anymore.

Just as he checked his watch for the umpteenth time in the last two hours the court usher stuck her head around the door.

'They're back,' she announced and disappeared.

Jack glanced at his watch, on this occasion registering the time. 4.15p.m. The jury had only been out for four hours.

He and Fabi entered the court and took up seats at the back. Jack surveyed the room. It was full. He spotted a couple of local reporters and gave them a weak smile. Jack could feel his stomach churning and this time it wasn't the pasty.

Kate Carty, CPS Barrister, turned to them and in a hopeful gesture issued a fingers crossed salute and then returned to face the bench.

Seconds later the jury room door opened and the twelve members began to slowly file in. As they took their seats Jack found himself scrutinising their faces anew, trying to anticipate the decision they had come to.

The court usher asked the foreman to rise. It was one of the women. She looked to be in her early fifties, with shoulder-length straight fair hair cut into a fringe. She straightened her dark grey slacks as she rose and then overlapped her hands in front of her.

'Ladies and Gentlemen of the jury have you agreed a verdict on which all of you agree?' asked the usher.

'We have'

'On the first count, the charge of the murder of Carrie Jefferies, do you find the defendant guilty or not guilty?'

38

A rousing applause greeted Jack and Fabi as they entered the CID office at Penzance. Every one of their team was on their feet wearing a beaming smile.

DI Dick Harrison stepped forward and touched Jack's arm, 'Well done. Great job. Twenty-two years' minimum sentence – that's a good result.'

Jack smiled and glanced sideways at Fabi. She wore a pleased but embarrassed look.

The DI shook Fabi's hand, 'There aren't many trainee detectives get a murder to deal with on their very first case. Congratulations.' After a brief pause he said, 'Don't take your coat off, the first rounds on me.'

***

Standing in the lounge of the pub holding an almost empty beer glass Jack viewed the celebration going on around the room with no emotion. It was the first time he had ever felt like this after a big case and it disturbed him. It was if he watching this from outside the building. He saw Fabi emerge from the bar carrying a fresh beer for him and a glass of white wine for herself. He knew it would be Prosecco. He had already learned it was her favourite tipple.

She handed him his pint. 'Did I do well?'

'You did okay, but you've still got a fair way to go though.' Jack watched her smile dissipate and then gave a short laugh, 'Only joking, put your face back on.'

Her face lit up again and she gently punched his arm, 'You rotter. Seriously though, did I do all right? I have to confess when they told me who I'd got for my mentor and the legend you were I was bricking it.'

Jack expression turned sheepish. 'Now you're embarrassing me. Seriously Fabi, you did brilliant. You're a natural. You're going to make a great detective. And I don't say that to everyone.'

'I know, I've been told. Thank you, that means so much. She leaned forward and kissed his cheek.'

Jack face reddened, 'Well it's a long time since a girl's made me blush.'

Fabi burst out laughing. Then, she said, 'Well what now. What happens when all the excitement dies down?'

'Probably a shit job to deal with.'

Fabi's eyes drifted away for a moment and then they locked onto Jack. 'I hope you don't mind me saying…'

He issued a half-smile, 'Even if I did, I know you're going to say it.'

'…Back there in the court. I didn't say it at the time, but yesterday you just didn't seem with it.' She dropped her voice, 'Did the case get to you, or were you thinking about Claire again?'

'Honest truth Fabi? Everything's getting to me. I know I've not been the same guy since I came back to work.'

'Too early, you think?'

He pondered on her question and replied, 'No I don't think it's that. Claire's death, or at least the manner of her death has got to me, there's no denying it. And deep down I blame myself for that, but I also blame the job as well. Do you know before we lost the baby we had everything mapped out? We were going to be a family, look forward to my early retirement and then use my pension to travel round the world. Now look at what I've got to look forward to.'

Fabi grabbed Jack's wrist, 'Come on Jack you're young enough to begin again. You don't have to retire if you don't want to.'

He pulled back his gaze, 'I know that Fabi, but I've had my good ride and now I think it's time to get off the roundabout.'

39

Jack sat hunkered over his desk, his eyes glued to the incident board, which hadn't yet been taken down. He was in the CID office alone, having left everyone else still celebrating at the pub. Half an hour earlier, having determined he wasn't in the frame of mind for a drinking session, he had taken Fabi to one side and whispered in her ear that he was off home, telling her he wanted to sneak away without any fuss and he asked her to cover for him. She said she understood and told him she'd see him in the morning, but as he stood outside, taking in the last of the warm evening, he changed his mind, deciding to grab some fish and chips and head back to the office to eat them before going home. He had done so, and now he was swilling them down with a mug of tea, letting his eyes drift around the photographs on the white board, flicking from Mathew's mug shot, to Carrie's burned out mini, and finally to the digital impression they had of Carrie, before repeating the process again. He had never known a case like this; a case where they hadn't managed to find out anything about the victim as well as not get closure for the victim's family. He hoped in the not too distant future someone will come forward and claim to be Carrie's parent or relative, and although he'd be unable to give them back her body, he'd at least be able to tell them they had got the person responsible for her murder. For a moment he stopped his thoughts there, locking eyes with Carrie's digital image. That niggling doubt he had felt many times during this enquiry had leaped into his thoughts again, but he couldn't understand why, especially after today's verdict. In fast-forward mode he played out the investigation inside his head, pausing at each key fact, and at each of the witness's testimonies, wondering if he had got any of it wrong. As he got to the end he knew he hadn't and yet something was gnawing away inside. He took a deep breath and pulled back his gaze, freeze-framing it at Fabi's desk where he spotted the coroner's file on Angel May's suicide. Could it be that case? He had to admit he had been extremely frustrated when CPS had informed him that the Judge had ruled that they could not present this evidence, after all Mathew had a hand in her death, albeit that they couldn't prove he had actually killed her. He leaned across, dragged the case papers toward him and unfastened the bundle. Then he began separating the paperwork. He had read through the file twice, but now that his thoughts took a different approach, he wondered if he'd find anything that he might have missed. There was certainly no harm in looking, he told himself as he picked out the first statement. An hour and half later, after only getting up from his desk once to switch on the lights, he had finished the file and sighed as he turned the last page. It was as he thought, he had missed nothing. He began to bunch it back together when he spied the digital newspaper headlines that Fabi had printed out and used as background information and he picked them up. Quickly scanning each copy there was one that took his interest. It was the funeral report with a cast of mourners around Angel's grave. He recalled what Fabi had said about the model's celebrity status and he began to search among the mourners faces to see which of them he could name. On the front row he picked out a couple of soap actors he recognised, although he couldn't recall their names and then he moved up to the second line. At the fourth face he stopped. There was something about the blonde haired woman he recognised, but he couldn't think why. He knew she wasn't a celebrity. Bending closer to the photograph he studied her image while searching his mind. It was something about the eyes and the nose, he thought. Then, in a flash, it came to him. Shaping fore-finger and thumb he covered part of her face and he instantly knew why she had grabbed his attention. Dropping the newspaper printout, he reached back to Angel's file – there were some documents at the back that he wanted to check through. He quickly found the records he wanted – they were printed across two pages – and scrolling down the list he found what he was looking for. Marking the spot with his finger he picked up the phone and tapped in a number. This would confirm everything.

Three months later...

40

Jack stopped off in Singapore and had three days of sight-seeing before hopping back on another plane to take him onto his destination of Australia. At Sidney airport he hired himself a top-end 4 x 4 and drove at a leisurely speed along the Great Western Highway for six hours to the final destination of his journey – Rockley. He had already researched the place before leaving England and learned that it was just a small village in the vastness of New South Wales with a population of just a few hundred people. With only one main road and a couple of long side roads he knew it wouldn't take him long to find the person he was looking for.

As he approached the outskirts he couldn't help but be impressed by the lushness of the surroundings, with rolling hills and shady parkland. It reminded him so much of his home county of Cornwall – but on a grander scale. Upon entering the village, he was even more impressed – it was a place where time had almost stood still. Either side of the thin stretch of road was either a porch-fronted wooden house or a homestead stereotypical of those he had seen in books during school geography lessons back in the early 1970s.

The house he was looking for was on Hill Street, and spotting the sign at a junction he dropped down two gears and took a left onto an even thinner stretch of tarmac and kept his speed slow. The number he wanted was a bungalow and, after passing a tree-lined rise, he zeroed in on a green painted single-storey wooden building perched above him, and he took his foot off the accelerator and cruised onto the grass verge which served as a parking area.

For five minutes he remained at the wheel with the engine idling, steadying his breathing as he stared up at the house. Although the bungalow was old, he could see it had been kept in good condition and the paintwork looked fresh. He was just admiring the bush of purple flowers cascading over the porch roof, wondering what they were, when the silhouette of a figure appeared at the window. It remained there for the best part of a minute and although Jack couldn't see the eyes he knew they were looking down at him. He turned off the engine, pushed open the car door and, stretching the cramp out of his legs, began his ascent up the stone steps leading to the bungalow. As he stepped onto the porch a mesh door opened outwards and a woman appeared in the doorway. She was the same blonde haired woman he had seen in the photograph of the mourners beside Angel May's grave.

'Caroline Jefferson?' he asked, stepping toward the door and, as he gripped the frame and stared into her intensely bright blue eyes added, 'Or should I say Carrie Jefferies?'

Her face remained expressionless. 'How did you find me?'

'It wasn't easy I can tell you. Can I come in?'

She walked back into the house without answering and Jack followed letting the mesh door swing back into place. Inside the kitchen, panelled walls were painted white and blue and the furniture was dark wood.

She went to the fridge and opened the door. 'Can I get you a cool beer?' she said without looking back.

'A beer would be great.' Jack answered.

The woman took out two beers, whipped off their tops, handed Jack one and then took a swig of her own. Wiping the back of her hand across her lips she said, 'So how did you find me?'

'It was fluke really. I happened to see a photo of Angel's funeral and you were one of the mourners.'

She gave Jack a meek smile and shook her head. 'And I thought I'd covered my tracks.'

'You had. Believe me. It was sheer luck I saw that photo in the paper. Your hair fooled me of course because it wasn't auburn like in Mathew's paintings, but your eyes gave you away. That was one thing Mathew captured in his paintings – your eyes.' He dipped his head toward her face, 'And he got them bang on.'

She seated herself at the kitchen table and presented Jack a chair opposite. 'There's one thing I'll say about Mathew he was a good painter.' She took another swig of her beer and, holding the neck of the bottle close to her bottom lip continued, 'But that's the only good thing I will say about him.' Then, pointing the bottle toward Jack she said, 'Recognising my photograph is one thing, tracking me down is another. How did you do that?'

'Your phone calls.'

'Phone calls?'

'Angel. I saw from her phone records that you used to ring her on a regular basis.'

Her heavy sigh was half laugh. 'My, you are a good detective.'

'Want to tell me about it. I think I know but I'd like you to tell me.'

She set her bottle down on the table. 'You know Angel's my sister?'

Jack nodded and took a drink of the cold beer. It was the best he'd tasted in a long time. 'I do now. It took me a while to find out, but after a couple of phone calls I got there in the end.'

'You know all about how we got separated?'

Jack nodded again, not removing the bottle from his mouth.

'So you know then that Mum and Dad got killed in an accident when I was eight and Angela was eighteen months old.' She paused, exchanged glances and continued, 'My aunt looked after us at first, but she'd already got the offer of a job here, and she decided she could only manage me because I was old enough, and so she left Angela with the Mayberry's who were her best friends. They couldn't have children and had always wanted one so it was the ideal solution. I, of course, was brought up here, and it was only when my aunt died of cancer five years ago that I was told exactly where Angela was. When I contacted her I discovered that she was a famous model. I couldn't believe it. I was so pleased for her and as you know we kept in touch regularly. She sent me money, paid for this house, and helped me buy a few luxuries and then we arranged for me to come across to London to stay with her. Then she started telling me about this artist she'd met – Mathew. She was so besotted with him, but after about six months I could tell on the phone that she was different. Not only acted different but sounded different – really down. She eventually told me that Mathew had got her into drugs and she was trying to stop. Then the next thing she told me was that Mathew had drugged and raped someone. I told her she had to end it, she told me she was going to and the next thing I saw on the news was that Angela was dead.'

'And you set out for revenge?'

'Not at first I didn't. I thought Mathew would be arrested. But then I discovered he'd got off.'

'The inquest said she committed suicide.'

She shook her head. 'Mathew was responsible for Angela's death.'

'And so you set out to get him.'

Dipping her head, she said, 'I didn't know exactly how initially. I just wanted to punish him, but first I needed to meet Mathew and find out about him. I'd managed to put some savings to one side, thanks to Angela's money, and once I got to England I did a bit of travelling for six months. During that time, I grew my hair longer, dyed it and changed my name. It wasn't hard finding Mathew and, guessing what type of person he was, I thought I'd have no difficulty in drawing him in. I wasn't wrong. It was just a matter of time before I worked out the best way of dealing with him.'

'And when did that idea come to you?'

'A lot of ideas came to me. I planned lots of things. I even tried to get him to talk about what had happened to Angel, which I taped, but all he would say about it was that it was a bad memory that he wanted to erase. You can imagine how that made me feel?'

'Furious?'

'You bet that. And that's when I knew that it needed some radical thinking. Then one night it came to me courtesy of the news. There was report on about this woman who'd disappeared, and who the police believed had been murdered, although they'd not found her body… and that was it. The seeds were sown.'

'And you put the plan into action that Sunday.'

Caroline gave a snort. 'That was pure luck. It happened because of an accident when I cut myself.'

'In the kitchen?'

She nodded. 'After I drove Mathew home that night from the Callaghan's we got back and he was still in a foul mood. At first I was going to sleep in the spare room and leave him to it, but he said he wanted another drink and told me to get him one. I said I thought he'd had enough and he just went crazy, started shouting and swearing at me. He threw those wine glasses across the kitchen and smashed them. He told me to pick them up, and that's when I cut myself. There I was on my hands and knees bleeding from a cut hand and the bastard just said I was fucking useless. He just went up to bed leaving me there. When I saw the blood dripping on the floor that's when I knew that the time was right.'

'Don't you feel guilty that Mathew has gone to prison for a murder he didn't commit.'

She laughed. 'He killed my sister didn't he? Not directly, but he was responsible for how she died and he got away with it. Now the scores settled.' She took a long drink of her beer. 'What happens now? Are you here to arrest me?'

Jack leaned back in the chair. 'Arrest you? I can't arrest you I'm not a detective anymore. I retired two months ago.'

***

After saying goodbye, Jack sat at the wheel of the 4 x 4 staring out through the windscreen, watching the heat haze rise from the tarmac and replaying in his head what he'd just heard. He thought about the decision he'd made to not contact the Australian Police and he knew that on this occasion the decision was right.

He started the car. He had got a long journey ahead. A long time to think. At least he had exorcised one ghost and he felt happier than he'd done in a long time.